MOTHMAN GOES WEST

WRITERS' WHEEL COLLECTIVE ANTHOLOGY

AMIEE NWABUIKE ANTONIO DINKENS

DAVID BADENCHINI EERIE MAEYFLOWER

GABRIEL PERAGINE MATT DWINELL

WRITERS' WHEEL COLLECTIVE

Book Cover by Angel Nwabuike

1st Edition 2026

CONTENTS

Mothman Begins His Journey

AMIEE NWABUIKE AND MATT DWINELL

A *sweet flavor, mildly acidic...* I hated to admit it, but it was good. It was *very* good. I took another reluctant sip of the swirling wine. I made sure to give nothing away on my face, but it didn't matter. Jersey looked as self-contented as always.

"Good, isn't it? Much better than the swill they squeeze out of mushrooms and beaver tails around here," Jersey said.

I bridled. "Point Pleasant is an excellent community. I'll have you know—"

Jersey cut me off. "And too bad. I tell you, the sights I see with all this fresh blood moving in. There's never a dull moment. Just the other day I conned some souls off a couple of traveling fancy pants. Thezpians, they called themselves. You should have seen them with their striped collars sticking all up in the air. I laughed so hard I practically made myself nausea."

He mispronounced the word "nausea" like it rhymed with "naughty," cackling while he did so for emphasis. "Mothy, you should come out to the South Shore sometime—I'll show you around. We've got a practical utopolis out there, better than skulking in the foggy hills all day. Truly, I can't imagine boring myself to tears out here."

Smug bastard, I thought to myself. Of course the stoic majesty of the Smoky Mountains would be lost on him.

I endured the Jersey Devil's abuse of my hospitality and patience for the next eight hours. He eventually departed with a click of cloven hooves and a flap of leathery wings, but his presence left an undeniable stain on my mental fortitude. Perhaps still under the influence of the extra wine he had gifted me, a seed was planted in my mind. I began to form a plan, or rather, a quest for revenge.

Disguised as a non-descript human traveler of a normal height of seven feet, I would journey westward. I would mingle with the mortal inhabitants and feast on the finest milk and honey the land had to offer. Who would be the rustic bumpkin then when Jersey came tapping back at my foothills? I gave a quiet *bzzzzzzz* of delight at the thought. And my first destination? A stop to the best wine on this side of Cthulhu's tentacled beard—Roanoke, North Carolina, for a sip of the Scuppernong Mother Vine.

THE SCUPPERNONG MOTHER VINE

AMIEE NWABUIKE

August winds stretched across the coast. They brought in a cool breeze and pushed waves of haint blue over the Roanoke Sound and into the swaying whispers of the creeping spike-rush. Seagulls and terns bobbed in the summer sky, catching the updraft like a ballet of dancing kites. Beneath the water, in the smaller creeks of the island, forests of eelgrass ebbed with the current. Minnows and young perch hovered and darted between the blades, their scales catching the sunlight in tiny flashes. To the children playing in the shallows, the fish seemed like meteors burning in the night sky as they dodged through fingers and around toes.

Over all of this, the scuppernong grape vines kept watch. Their roots ran from one sandy shore of the island to the other. They grew freely in the freshwater marshes, and even in the town square, a stray tendril could be found poking out between the cobblestones. Around the corpse of old Fort Roanoke, their leaves grew thickest, choking any sound from reaching the empty beds and kitchen tables long abandoned there. Which is why the vines felt the vibrations of clumsy footsteps all the way through the forest, long before three figures stumbled out of the tree line and into the clearing of Fort Roanoke with shovels and canvas sacks in tow.

The one in front motioned to the other two. "We'll split up and look through the houses first. You come across any tombstones, start digging."

The man beside him shifted nervously, trying to ignore the horsefly bites swelling on the back of his neck. "But why would there be any graves if the settlers disappeared like the islanders said?" he asked.

The man bringing up the rear hocked a thick, black wad of chewing tobacco onto the ground. "These island rubes don't know sense from superstition," he said. "No settlers disappeared. Bet you they just got attacked by some natives," he continued as he unwrapped the last bit of his tobacco plug and placed it in his mouth.

The first man laughed in agreement. "We'll probably find a pit of scalps somewhere. Hopefully buried with some English gold." He noticed his nervous companion still looking uncertain and gave him a hearty slap on the back. "Don't believe those ghost stories! By tonight we'll either have something to pay for every drink in town or a pilgrim skull to chase the local girls around with."

Their grave robbing ambitions would remain just that, however. Before they even finished the final steps to the Fort Roanoke gate, the earth split open beneath their feet. Grape vines poured out of the open gashes of soil. Up and out, before the men could even register a shout, boughs, branches, and curling tendrils engulfed them. Their arms and legs became wrapped in the vines, and the sinewy limbs hardened in place, holding them fast. And then the vines began to pull. Down into the cold darkness. Down into the waiting rootstock. Down into the soil all three went.

As they descended, the nervous man happened to catch a break in the foliage covering his face. He still could not move, but with the last bit of light, he glanced something between the grape leaves. Waiting for him and his friends were more bodies buried into the sides of the earth. But unlike him and his companions, these were desiccated corpses. Vegetation sprouted through where fingernails and eye sockets should have been—the leathery skin and vines so intertwined, one could no longer tell where either began or ended. Then the ground closed up above him, and the man saw nothing at all.

On the surface, the earth stitched itself back together. Nothing was left but a few rows of tilled soil. Within a few days, the grass would grow over it again, and after a couple of rainfalls, a passerby would never know anything had happened there at all. Already, the thick silence returned to the corpse of old Fort Roanoke. It choked any sound from reaching the empty beds and kitchen tables long abandoned there. And over all of this, the scuppernong grape vines kept watch.

Three miles down the coast from Fort Roanoke, the mayor's vineyard was bustling with activity. Under the summer sun, the scuppernong vines were heavy with clusters of fruit. Each grape was swelling into a perfect, golden orb. Some were so ripe that cracks were opening in their thick skins. The bees and wasps were beside themselves with the intoxicating scent of the vineyard, which you could smell downwind all the way into town. To the farmhands working their way down the rows, it was obvious this would be one of the best harvests yet for the island.

None of this, however, was impressive to one particular farmhand: Ottavio "Otto" Hartcastle. He snuck through the vegetation with one hand on his straw boater hat, keeping it pressed firmly on his head of short, black curls. With his other hand, he picked his way through the rows. He was careful to keep his waistcoat from getting stained with grape juice and sap. This waistcoat came with a matching pair of tweed trousers made on the mainland. Otto had acquired it with great effort from a passing traveler by persuading him to trade for a Johnny Doe Bible that Otto had inherited from his father. As soon as the fabric had touched his fingers, Otto knew that he would kill a man before he would part with this waistcoat.

His dark eyes scanned down the vineyard rows as he searched for his compatriot. Being spotted by the wrong farmhand would sentence him to some kind of odious labor for the rest of the day, and Otto had no time for distractions. His efforts bore fruit as he spotted a stout figure in overalls swinging a basket of grapes overhead. It was Clancy Matthews. He was one year younger than Otto, and the two of them had been bosom friends since a dysentery outbreak had left them both toddler orphans.

"Psst! Clance!" Otto hissed from behind a wall of leaves.

Clancy put down his basket and looked through the foliage where Otto's lanky, brown face stared up at him.

"Otto? Where you got to?" Clancy said with a laugh of surprise. "The mayor was here lookin' for you earlier, but lucky I picked your share of rows already. If you help me with this last basket, we can ask the other hands if they need any help."

Otto looked at Clancy with horror, reeling at the thought that he not only wanted to finish his work but everyone else's as well. This was what he considered to be one of Clancy's two greatest shortcomings: a misplaced devotion to farm work that created a complete contentment with mundanity.

"Clancy! There's no time for farm chores," Otto admonished him. "Leave the grapes. I've stumbled onto an entrepreneurial endeavor that can fund our way West in an evening."

Clancy pulled an old rag out of his overall pocket and soaked up the back of his neck.

"I dunno, Otto," he said in no particular hurry. "The scuppernongs are ripe for pickin', and we still gotta set up the barn for the festival and all."

"These bloated grapes will be here whether we pick them or not, but these tourists are only passing by for the weekend, Clance. Can't you see that now is the time to strike? If we let fortune slip through our fingers like this, what fools would we be?"

Clancy regarded him with lazy skepticism. Ever since they were children, Clancy had always recognized an ambition and creativity in Otto that he admired. But he could also recognize a harebrained plot when he heard one. Usually, he would still join such misadventures out of simple curiosity. On this occasion, however, his sense of responsibility prevented even that from swaying him.

Sensing his friend's recalcitrance, Otto resorted to stronger measures.

"Clancy, are you really going to slave away picking grapes just to have a measly sawbuck at the end of the year to show for it? We're never going to be anything more than orphan farmhands if we stay stuck on this island. But out West we have a chance to make a name and a fortune for ourselves." Otto moved in for the kill: "And how are you ever going to have a chance of winning the hand of a lady like Ms. Lottie with farmhand wages?"

Clancy's mood changed immediately. "Aww shucks. You're right, Otto."

Otto nodded sagely, and the two of them began sneaking their way out of the vineyard, leaving the abandoned basket of grapes under the watch of the scuppernong vines.

The morning ferry pulled up to the Roanoke Island dock, dropping off its bundle of tourists from the mainland. As they stepped onto the boardwalk, they were greeted by the beach breeze, the sweet scent of wild scuppernong grapes ripening everywhere, and a wooden stall where Otto had set up his new business venture. A giant, hand-painted sign was fastened above the booth. "Lost Colony Curios" it read in bold letters.

Naturally, the tourists gathered around it immediately. Otto leaned out of the stall to welcome them, his fashionable waistcoat sticking out like the plumage of a tropical bird. He scanned the crowd and set his eyes on the tallest figure in the group. The man was easily a good head and shoulders above the rest, but even without his height, he would have stuck out. Whereas the other travelers were adorned with double-breasted vests and cheery colored parasols, the strange tourist was wearing a full-length black coat. His face was obscured by a wide-brimmed hat, under which two red eyes almost seemed to glow.

"Sir! Can I ask you a question?" Otto called.

The strange tourist pointed a hesitant finger at himself as the others looked at him with curiosity.

"Yes, you," Otto said while waving him over. "Judging by your posture and your fine cut of linen, it's my bet that you've come over from the mainland."

The tourist nodded in surprise. "Why yes," he agreed as he came closer.

A pensive finger to his lip, Otto looked him over for a few

seconds more before speaking again. "And I'm guessing that you're here for our summer festival."

"Wh-why yes! Correct again," the man said with delight as the crowd murmured.

"Then you're in luck!" Otto said. "Because I have here marvels of island history that you won't find anywhere else."

Seeing that he had the man's full attention along with the rest of the crowd, Otto flashed his best smile. "Sir, you stand on the very soil where one of our country's greatest mysteries took place. Let me ask you, what do you know about the Lost Colony of Roanoke?"

"I'm afraid I've never heard of it," the man said. Meanwhile, the people in the crowd glanced among themselves, equally unsure.

"Then let me tell you," Otto began. "This story starts three hundred years ago, when one hundred twenty English settlers dragged their sea-ravaged bodies from their battered ship right onto this very shore. They had barely escaped the monarchy with their lives, and most of them didn't even make it halfway across the Atlantic. But for the ones who hadn't succumbed to scurvy and pirates, they became the very first settlers on the continent."

A murmur of awe rippled through the crowd. Otto continued.

"The first thing they did was strike up an alliance with the native Secotan tribes. With their help, they built log by log, hand by hand, the impenetrable Fort Roanoke." Like every person on the island, Otto had heard this story a hundred times over from a young age. And while he did have most of the technical facts correct, he helped himself to a creative liberty or two. "What you must understand is that Fort Roanoke was an engineering marvel of the sixteenth century. Its sturdy walls were so high, so thick, the settlers should have been protected from all attack—whether from man or beast in the strange new world they called home. And with all the aid the Secotan natives gave them, they were feasting from the fat of the land. That is why when General White returned three years later with fresh supplies and a new group of settlers, he expected to be greeted by healthy, happy colonists. But what did he find instead?"

Otto stopped here, and the man and the crowd looked at him eagerly, unsure of what to expect next.

"Nothing at all," Otto said at last. "Yes, Fort Roanoke was still there, but not a single settler was inside. Fully made meals were still on the table, uneaten. Sets of clothes were still left on the bed, clean and unwrinkled. Empty cribs were still rocking in the breeze. The entire place was deserted but untouched, like every living soul there had been raptured off the earth."

"My God!" said the tourist. "Did they ever find them?"

Otto shook his head sadly. "To this day, no one knows what became of the one hundred twenty settlers. Not a single grave, body, or lock of hair was ever found."

A concerned whisper went through the crowd. Some of them threw around theories among themselves. Starvation? Animal attack? Sorcery?

From the front of the crowd, a young girl raised a hand. Otto turned to her.

"Yes?" he asked.

"What happened to the Secotans?" the little girl asked.

The question caught him off guard as he realized he had no clue. None of his schoolteachers had ever mentioned anything more about them, even in the few minutes when he could be bothered to pay attention to said teachers. Even the mayor had never spoken more about them, and no one knew more about the island and long speeches than he did.

"Well, the records are not clear, exactly," Otto stumbled a

little. "But after helping the kind settlers, we can only assume that the Secotans left the island and went to go live somewhere else."

The little girl and the rest of the crowd looked at him uncertainly. Otto cleared his throat loudly to gather their attention. "While no trace of the settlers ever came about, they did leave many things behind before whatever unknown end sealed their fate. And I have one of those artifacts here for you today." With a flourish, Otto whipped out a small glass bottle. Inside, a collection of little, white objects rattled around.

"Recovered directly from the site of Fort Roanoke, these are the teeth of the first babies born on American soil!"

The crowd gasped.

"That's right, ladies and gentlemen," Otto yelled triumphantly. "For just a nickel, you can hold a relic of the Lost Colony in your very own hands and own a piece of our country's history."

Wallets and handbags opened eagerly as the tourists pushed to the front of the stall. Unbeknownst to them, beneath the boardwalk, Clancy was busy whittling seashells into the shapes of little molars and incisors, a nice surplus of bottled teeth growing around him.

Otto barely got to enjoy the feel of the first nickel in his hand before an adamantine voice cut through the excited crowd around him.

"Lord's mercy!" the voice of the mayor called out. The man was toeing the age of gray hair and dimming eyes, but his voice could carry across a room as powerfully as it ever had. "I cannot have a moment's rest with you two," he cried as he cut to the front of the line.

"Ottavio, what is all this? Lost Colony Curios?" He held up one of the bottles and scowled as if the force of his gaze would make the contents confess their identity.

"They're baby teeth, sir," the strange tourist offered helpfully.

The mayor clutched his heart and gave a pained yell. With a sigh, Otto returned the nickel to the still open hand of his first customer. He had the foresight to know where this was headed.

The crowd disbanded as the mayor launched into a diatribe about the dangers of greed and avarice. By the time he finished, the people had long made their way off the boardwalk and to the safety of officially sanctioned festival activities.

After enduring the mayor's lectures and lamentations about their crimes, Otto and Clancy were banished back to the vineyard and tasked with setting up the barn for wine tastings. Thus they spent the long afternoon hauling wine barrels, pouring samplers, and regaling the history of the island for the umpteenth time (for no extra charge, much to Otto's despair). After several hours of such profitless torture, the crowds lulled as the tourists moved on to the evening festivities set up in the town square. With nothing to do, Clancy gathered up a handful of nodding lady tresses, which he happened to know was Lottie's favorite flower, and began picking petals idly. Meanwhile, Otto let himself be consumed with all manner of dark ruminations. After some time like this, he broke the silence between them.

"Clancy, I've figured out the secret behind our rotten misfortunes. Cannibals, Clancy. That's what it was."

Clancy, absorbed with his petals, gave him a half-glance but said nothing.

Otto continued, "Think, your grandfather and mine were both whalers. They would have left their homes in search of ambergris—the gold of the sea. Mine was probably the captain of the ship, while your ancestor was likely a lowly cabin boy hoping to work his way up in the world."

"Cabin boy?" Clancy repeated with a lazy nod as a growing mound of fluff fell around him.

"Yes. They would have sailed the Atlantic, beaching and harpooning whales in fountains of blood until they found themselves in strange waters off the coast of Argentina where they were beset by a crazed humpback."

"Mmm, crazed," Clancy sighed dreamily.

"The beast would have torn their ship to pieces, leaving the crew stranded in nothing but a leaking rowboat, miles out at sea." At this point, Otto's eyes were lit up with visions that only he could see. He clutched at his throat. "Their lips cracked with thirst, fingernails black with malnourishment, desiccated skin clinging to their bones—they would die off from exposure and hunger slowly, slowly. They would bury the first bodies honorably at sea, but as the days turn to weeks, their insatiable hunger would drive them mad, and they would devour the green, sickly flesh of their dead crewmates, raw and cold."

Otto slammed a fist down on the countertop. His eyes gazed at the barn walls where barrels of wine were stacked, but in his mind he was in the languid waves of the Atlantic, hearing the sound of rotted teeth tearing through gangrene flesh.

"Just as your grandfather would have been begging mine to put him out of his misery and take his lifeforce to survive, they would have been rescued by a naval ship and returned home. But the shame of their sinful deeds would have made them social pariahs, banned from all civilized society and spurned by God himself."

Otto shut his eyes painfully and took in a deep breath. "*That*, Clancy, is how they must have come to settle on this hayseed island and bring their cursed luck down upon all their children and us. It's the only logical explanation I can think of."

Having laid out his theory, Otto turned to look at Clancy, expecting to find him awestruck in horror by this evident truth. He was disappointed to see that Clancy had no look on his face even close to awe or horror, but simply a full pile of petals lying around him.

"Clancy, what *are* you doing?"

Realizing that Otto had finished his story, Clancy spoke at last, "Otto, which do you think is more romantic? A beachside wedding or a barn side wedding?"

Dismayed, Otto drew his breath in sharply, collecting his thoughts.

"Clance, every day I worry about the state of your mind. Here we are standing face to face with the foremost turmoil of our youths and the very battle for our futures and souls, and you are sitting there asking me about barn side weddings!"

"Well, say that we make our way west—I should know how much I need to save up for when we get out there. A beach sunset would really suit the flecks of gold in Ms. Lottie's eyes. But with a barn side wedding, I could rent a horse and carriage for her entrance."

Otto let out a long sigh. Moments like this confirmed what he diagnosed as Clancy's main affliction of character: a completely oversexed mind. And yet, Otto couldn't stay mad at such earnest enthusiasm.

"You should have a barn side wedding, Clance. You have to remember that all your guests will be from this island. A beachside wedding won't capture their imagination like the novelty of a barn side vista. And with a barn side wedding, you can bring in more flowers to go with—" he paused, taking some courage to get the last words out, "Miss Lottie's eyes."

Clancy broke into an ear-to-ear grin. "Otto, you always have the best ideas!"

Otto shook his head in agreement, but quietly resigned himself. There would be no reaching Clancy with any sense for the next hour. He would instead be daydreaming about guest placement and which flowers matched with Lottie's wedding dress for the remainder of their work shift.

Thankfully, the painful boredom on the horizon was interrupted by a newcomer at the door. The smell of scuppernongs wafted in strongly as Otto recognized the strange tourist from earlier that morning. The man had to duck to avoid hitting his head on the threshold, and he moved with a shuffling gate, as if he was dragging something large and cumbersome behind him, like a rolled-up carpet. Otto's mood lifted. Perhaps here he would find a tourist worth talking to and something to break up the doldrum of the afternoon.

"Sir, I believe I know your secret," Otto said with a smile as the man came up to the counter.

The stranger seemed to panic. "Secret? What secret? I am simply a nondescript human traveler of a normal height of seven feet." His eyes flashed a wider red.

Otto swept out a hand as he looked him up and down. "Your clothes, your physique, the enigmatic composure that surrounds you—you must hark from the Europine countries, am I right?"

The man calmed down and let out a peculiar, buzzing laugh. "HooOOooOOooh. Not at all! I'm from a little gem of a town in the Smoky Mountains; Point Pleasant—"

The stranger did not get a chance to finish his sentence. "Sir, samples are along the side of the room. Complimentary nuts and cheeses are in the icebox," Otto said with a friendly but dismissive wave.

The stranger shuffled away, deflated, and Otto shook his

head. Another common yokel tourist. This all but confirmed his cannibal theory.

As the strange tourist left to swirl sparkling muscadine in his tasting glass, his gloomy presence was replaced by an even stranger creature: Lottie Baum. She was the same twenty-one years as Clancy, so he had often seen her around the island as they were growing up. As the mayor's daughter and only child, she was essentially town royalty. Even without that title she could have been the belle of any town, maybe even of a modestly populated city. Her golden hair hung in long curls, tied up on either side of her head by chiffon bows. And while Otto was not bewitched by them, he could see how a man or woman of a weaker constitution could become wrapped up in Lottie's doe-brown eyes. All of this was complemented by the dresses her father had imported for her. Presently, she was wearing a summer dress over her dainty frame, complete with a lace chemisette and pagoda sleeves.

But while her appearance was that of any young debutante, what Otto found strange about her was nearly everything else. She had a habit of collecting frogs, twigs, and owl pellets, which she could produce from her handbag without warning. She also had a peculiar walk where she would stop and gasp quietly to herself, like a strand of lightning had just whispered to her. Otto had on occasion talked to her, and he found that Lottie had absolutely no appreciation for hyperbole or metaphor (a grave disappointment). He could only wonder what business she had in the barn. He glanced over at Clancy to see if he had any insights. He saw that Clancy had fallen off the barrel he was sitting on and was scrambling to hide his collection of flower petals. Otto turned his attention back to their new guest.

"Ms. Baum! To what do we owe the pleasure?" Otto said with what he considered a dazzling smile.

Lottie looked at him with shock. “To nothing. There’s no charge for me being here,” she stated matter-of-factly.

Otto held back a sigh. If he had not known Lottie better, he would have thought she was mocking him, but there was nothing but genuine concern in her gaze. He thought about his words for a moment before responding carefully. “Is there anything I can help you with, Ms. Lottie?” Otto asked.

Lottie hung the crook of her pink parasol on one arm and reached into her pouch with her free hand, pulling out a small piece of fabric that she held up to Otto. He examined it and saw daintily embroidered words: “Tourists Missing. Contact Constable.”

Seeing his quizzical look, Lottie explained. “A mainlander went missing at the summer festival last year, and two more the year before that. Despite this, my father hasn’t done anything to locate them.”

“I understand your concern,” Otto said, “but what makes you so certain they’re missing? How do you know they didn’t leave on the last ferry with everyone else?”

“I had suspicions after the first festival. For the next few weeks, I noticed that the grapes were showing a copper tinge on their skins. And their taste was altered—slightly more acidic than usual, like a large deposit of iron had gotten into the roots. And our wildlife was acting peculiar, too. Here, I could show you some owl pellets I collected, if you like,” Lottie said while reaching for her handbag.

Otto’s hands shot up in alarm, motioning her to stop. “That won’t be necessary,” he said hastily. He thought quickly of how he could draw her attention away from any owl pellets. “Ms. Lottie, those are all excellent observations, but I’m not sure that adds up to missing tourists.”

“Well, there’s that, and I also heard the screams under the island,” Lottie said simply.

Otto's eyebrows shot up. "Screams?"

"Yes, during the festivals. It was like someone was being dragged underground."

Otto decided that some things were better left untouched. Changing the subject, he motioned to the little square of fabric that Lottie had handed him earlier. "And these are?" he asked.

"I embroidered these to raise awareness. We can tie them around the wine bottles. That way when people come to buy some, they'll be informed about the missing tourists."

"And how many of these do you have?" Otto asked.

"Ten that I've made so far," Lottie said.

"That's very noble of you, Ms. Lottie. I'm sure my insouciant friend here can have these doilies attached post haste." Otto motioned toward Clancy.

They both turned to look at where Clancy had finally finished tripping over himself. He was now standing like his spine had turned into an iron rod and seemed to be paralyzed between several different emotions and expressions all at once.

"Oh, is this your friend?" Lottie said. "I thought that was an insane person."

The sun was getting low in the sky, but the Festival was still in full swing at the town square. The gas lamps on the street corners were flickering to life, and a variety of stalls were on display around the plaza. There were booths with carnival games and booths handing out paper boats and pinwheels for the children, and there was no shortage of food. Crab cakes, shrimp and grits, corn bread, poke sallet—every dish the island had to offer was being served up around the square. At the end of the plaza, a stage had been set up. A band was playing an up-tempo "Buffalo Gals," and the sound of music mixed with the sizzle and seasoning of island cooking in the air.

Otto was at one of the food booths, ordering some fried snapper and a turkey leg drizzled in butter, spice, and sweet scuppernong gravy. He regaled the cook with the tale of how he and Clancy had worked in the vineyard all day, staving off throngs of wine-crazed tourists for a measly pittance. His story was enough to get him an extra helping of gravy, and with his hoard of food, he made his way across the cobblestone street to where Clancy was sitting on the curb.

"Look, Clance," Otto said as he waved the drumstick around his nose. "I've got your favorite—and extra gravy to go with it!"

Clancy took the drumstick but made no move to try it.

Otto sat down next to him and put a concerned hand on his back. "My goodness, Clance. What's wrong?"

Clancy gave a loud groan. "I ruined it all. My best chance to talk with Ms. Lottie, and I plum blew it."

"You're still upset about that?" Otto asked.

Clancy's despondent stare gave him his answer.

Otto regarded his forlorn friend. "What has you so besotted with Lottie Baum anyways?" he asked.

Clancy blushed. "Oh, I don't know..." he trailed off.

Otto stomped his foot hard on the pavement. The sudden noise and movement made Clancy jerk to attention.

"No hemming and hawing!" Otto demanded. "I've watched you tie yourself in knots over this girl for years. Now answer me straight!"

Clancy squirmed for a few moments, but seeing the look on Otto's face, he finally relented. "I-I guess what I like about Ms. Lottie is that she knows more about the island than anyone else. Even though I've lived here my whole life, she'll still find something that surprises me. Like today—I noticed the grapes had gone coppery last year. But I had never thought to ask why, and I never even noticed the taste changed. And you know I get my words all tied up when I have to talk in front of a bunch of people. But Lottie never cares what anyone thinks. She'll tell you what she has to say plain and honest just the way she sees it."

Clancy shook his head and let out a sigh. "I guess that's what I like most about her. She's smart and brave. Like you, Otto."

Having finished his speech, Clancy at last turned to his turkey leg, taking a half-hearted bite as he idly watched the dancing in the square. Meanwhile, Otto sat in stunned silence. He shifted uncomfortably. He had not expected such sincerity from Clancy's answer, and he was beginning to feel a twinge of guilt. Clancy had the impression that they would make names and fortunes for themselves out West so he could return to Roanoke and win Lottie's heart. And while Otto did expect to make a name and fortune for them both, he figured that Clancy would abandon this attachment to provincial life and romance once they embarked. Hearing Clancy talk like this, Otto couldn't help but wonder: Was it wrong to take Clancy West? Would he be happier living his days here as a simple grape farmer?

Otto banished the thoughts from his head. No one would be happier living on this hayseed island where nothing happened, he reminded himself. He sprang to his feet. "All the more reason to head West, my friend!" he said with renewed energy. "We may only have a few spondulicks to our name, but once we get out there, everything will be better, you'll see."

Otto had planned to elaborate on the sights and adventures that awaited them, but he was cut short. A red-cheeked, boisterous man stumbled into him suddenly. He would have knocked Otto over if Clancy hadn't caught him and saved both

Otto and his waistcoat from falling into the trash and dirt behind them.

The drunken man righted himself. "Hey-ooh! Stable boys. Excellent imbibage!" He held up a bottle of wine and shook it back and forth, spilling drops everywhere.

"Gracious, Clance," Otto said as he performatively dusted himself off. "These mainlanders are even drunker than last year—shiftless lounge-abouts."

Clancy looked around them. Strewn about the square was a day's worth of tourist mementos. Half-eaten turkey legs and crab cakes that children had dropped were lying on the streets. Gnawed corn cobs were tossed in the bushes, and a fleet of wine corks were bobbing in the town fountain along with an inexplicably discarded boot. "Plenty more to clean up this year too," Clancy said as he surveyed the damage.

Otto shook his head in distaste. "I'm sure the mayor will be richer with all the wine we sold for him, but they won't even let us pawn a few baby teeth to these drunken louts."

The music from the band stopped, and everyone's attention was turned to the stage. As if summoned by Otto's complaints, the mayor walked out waving his hand in big, broad sweeps.

"Good evening y'all!" he bellowed from the front of the stage. "Is everyone having a good time?"

Cheers and shouts rang out from around the square.

The mayor laughed heartily to himself. "Glad to hear it. Remember that if you buy a crate of wine to take home, it gets better with age and you save a quarter on five."

Otto rolled his eyes.

The mayor continued to address the crowd. "And now we've got a special treat tonight. This island has a long, proud history, and my daughter has put together a little reenactment, a dramatic reading if you will, of the founding of Roanoke."

Otto had to stifle a laugh. He could only assume this was the mayor's scheme. With her practical nature, Lottie was the last person who would volunteer to do a dramatic reading of anything.

On cue, Lottie walked across the stage. She was still in her fine summer dress, though she had left her parasol and the bag of owl pellets behind. She did not seem put off by the crowd of eyes on her as she began to speak.

"Thank you all for coming to the Summer Harvest Festival. Before I get to the history of Roanoke, I want to remind you that if you know of any missing persons you should speak to the constable."

The mayor interjected, his face flushed with panic as he waved his hands in front of him. "Of course we want you all to stay safe, but there's no need to get riled up about anyone missing. That is—no one is missing at all!"

"Father, I think there are actually several people missing, from what I've seen."

The mayor was no doubt regretting his decision to give Lottie a platform. He turned to her in exasperation. "Lottie! We've already discussed this," he said tersely.

Lottie opened her mouth to say something more, but the mayor cut her off.

"For the last time, there is nothing to be alarmed about!"

At that moment, disaster struck. In attempting to share his drink with a hitched-up horse, a drunken tourist ended up drenching it in wine. Startled, the horse bucked. It kicked one of the gas lantern poles, and the whole thing went toppling down. The glass shattered, and the flame inside escaped. It caught easily on the azalea bushes that were already greased up with discarded turkey legs.

For one perfect moment, time seemed to stand still. The crowd watched, transfixed, as the shrubbery began to steadily burn brighter. It was the strange tourist who made the first move. He stood up silently from his wooden table, abandoning the plates of food he had been sampling there. His long coat dropped to the ground, and as it fell, dark wings spread out behind him. What stood there was the semblance of a man but covered in sooty bristle that wasn't quite fur and wasn't quite feathers. With a push of his wings, he took off into the night sky.

The sight of him flapping away from the disaster finally broke the spell over the crowd.

"That European bastard's getting away!" a voice yelled.

"He left us here to die!" another person screamed.

"We're all going to burn!"

The square erupted into chaos. Tourists tried to scatter, but the sober people found themselves tripping over trash and their more inebriated neighbors.The mayor's cries to form orderly lines were drowned out in a sea of shouts, panicked and confused. The festival vendors were scrambling to either escape their stalls or find something to calm the growing blaze. Some of them were simply stuck in place, trying to determine if they should join the firefighting efforts or run while they still could.

"We have to get out of here!" Otto yelled while tugging Clancy's sleeve.

"We gotta put out this fire!" Clancy said at the same time.

Before they had a chance to argue, they were cut off by a booming voice.

"ENOUGH!" it bellowed from beneath their feet, and the ground shook under the whole square. The earth split and an overgrowth of scuppernong roots and foliage swarmed forward. They engulfed the bushes, and between the vines and the upheaved dirt, the flames were finally smothered. But the vines did not stop there. They continued to grow out from the grass and dirt surrounding the plaza. They climbed up the food stalls, wrapped around the wooden tables, and stitched themselves together over the road, trapping everyone in the square. The stage where the band had been playing minutes before was completely overtaken as the scuppernong became a solid wall of knotted branches and leaves there.

"First you drunken boors foul my land with your waste, then you have the gall to set fire to *my* island?" The phantom voice echoed from the stage. The sound of it was like a thousand rustling whispers laid over each other, and it was both thunderous and creeping.

Otto was still holding on to Clancy's sleeve, and he tugged at it frantically now. "Clancy, are those plants on stage speaking or was there something in that gravy?"

Clancy shook his head. "No, I hear it too," he said.

Otto glanced around the crowd and saw that every face was looking in the same direction.

"It was a mercy I let this obscene farce go on for even one summer. But my patience is worn through," the vines declared. "None of you rotten tourists will live to see the morning!"

Moaning figures suddenly sprouted from the earth, and the revelers stared at them in horror. They were humanoid but had melded with the scuppernong. Some were nothing more than skulls and teeth peeking out between knotted greenery. Others still had scraps of flesh and muscle sinew grafted into splintering bark. They stumbled forward, gargling on decaying vocal cords as they stepped onto the cobblestones. With tendril hands and fingers, the swarm of reanimated corpses began to chase the screaming tourists. The ones unlucky enough to be caught were dragged toward the soil, where the gaping maws of earth and vines were waiting to claim them.

"Otto, do something!" Clancy begged as he looked at the turmoil around them.

Otto stared at him incredulously, not sure if he had heard correctly. "*Me*? What do you want me to do against a demon grape vine and a horde of plant corpses?" Otto asked, trying to keep his voice down. So far, the vine monsters had left the island locals untouched, but Otto did not want to chance drawing their attention and changing their minds.

"We can't just let the scuppernongs take all these people," Clancy said.

"I'm sorry, but even with the largest pair of pruning shears, our best bet is to wait this out and dig them up in the morning," Otto said.

"They won't last 'til morning!" Clancy protested. "But you could try talking to the vines up there."

"Talk to them? Clancy, do you hear yourself?" Otto whispered furiously. "Why would a demon vine listen to me?"

Around them, tourists continued to scream and flee—trying to escape the clawing tendrils and grasping vines but finding fewer and fewer places to run. Ignoring the chaos, Clancy looked at Otto solemnly. "Because you're the smartest person I know. You can convince a man to trade you the clothes off his back, and I know you can talk your way in or out of anything!"

Otto looked up at the coiling vines ahead of them, still unsure.

"And besides," Clancy said, "how can we say we're gonna find adventure out West if we can't even help with the one right in front of us?"

Otto closed his eyes and let Clancy's words sink in. He shook his head as he let out a painful sigh. "I don't know what scares me more. That I'm actually considering this or that you're the one doing the convincing now." He looked back at Clancy. "If we die here, I won't forgive you, you know," Otto complained but started walking toward the stage all the same. Clancy beamed and followed behind him.

With a deep breath, Otto cleared his throat and shouted toward the writhing mass of vines on stage.

"Excuse me! Your, um, Vine-ness?" Otto said.

There was no face or features in the scuppernongs, but Otto could feel the mass pause and regard him. Somehow, it was able to see and hear him, and Otto had to suppress shuddering at the thought. Having gotten its attention, Otto pushed forward.

"I couldn't help but notice you seem rather agitated..."

There was no answer from the scuppernong, but its assault on the tourists slowed. Otto continued.

"Let me apologize for the fire earlier. I'm sure that must have startled you, but we're all very thankful for your help quelling those flames. I know I speak for everyone here when I say I've never seen such an adroit display of leafage. And if you could kindly unhand the tourists, I know they would be happy to clean up this mess for you and let you get back to..." Otto paused, trying to think of what grape vines enjoyed. "Back to resting your roots in some nice, warm soil."

Around the square, the tourists were still caught fast in tangles of grape growth, but they were no longer being dragged toward the chasms in the earth. The Vine was still quietly fixated on Otto. He tried not to fidget under the weight of its silence as he spoke.

"And after all, you wouldn't want to tarnish the name of your beloved Summer Harvest Festival, would you?" he asked.

The Vine reacted suddenly. An undulating wave rippled through its leaves, and it made a sound like the rasp of a rusty pipe. As the brittle creaking surrounded him, Otto realized that it was laughing. He immediately wished he could go back to the inscrutable silence.

"Please! This Festival means nothing," the Vine spoke at last.

Otto shook his head. "There must be some misunderstanding," he protested, hoping he didn't sound as out of breath as he felt. "This Festival celebrates all the best parts of our island! People cross the channel just to hear the tale of our Lost Colony and get even a sip of your delicious scuppernong wine." Otto swept his arms out to gesture to the whole crowd. "In fact, I'm sure there's not a mainlander here who hasn't been illuminated by the celebrations this weekend."

The Vine slammed its weight against the stage abruptly, and Otto flinched at the sound of cracking bark and snapping boughs. "Don't mock me!" the Vine commanded, its voice booming again. "I know you, Ottavio," the Vine said, and Otto's skin grew clammy at the sound of his name. "I've felt every step you've taken since you first waddled on your feet. I've watched over you and every person on this island centuries before you were born." There was a pause, as if the Vine was considering something. "I know you hate this island," it said at last. "These mainlanders come here and you're more than happy to feed them lies, same as everyone else."

"Lies?" Otto asked hesitantly. Sweat dripped down his back. He wondered how much the Vine knew about his baby teeth venture from this morning.

The Vine shifted on stage, branches creaking as it moved. "Since you're so curious, before I bury these oafs in the ground, I'll illuminate you and everyone else here on the *true* history of Roanoke." As if settling into itself, the Vine curled and unfurled it leaves. It left the tourists dangling and fidgeting mid-grasp as its voice filled the square.

"Centuries ago, I was nothing more than a wild little marsh vine—fighting the roots of bigger trees, struggling through the freeze each winter, and battling off pests each summer. I was almost wiped out by a bad outbreak of root borers one season. That's when the Secotan people found me. They saved my seeds and scraggly shoots and brought me back from the brink of extinction.

"They picked the grubs off my leaves in the spring. They covered my roots with pine needles to keep me warm when the air chilled. With their help, I grew into a proper vine. I had new grafts and seedlings and rows of grape clusters larger and sweeter than ever before. I felt the Secotan children play between my leaves. I watched them grow old and be buried with my roots. I was with them through every cold winter and every bad storm. But even when the weather was hard, each autumn, I was still happy to grow more grapes than they could eat."

The Vine paused its story here, apparently caught up in some memories only it could see. It was fully dark now, and a cool breeze was rustling the scuppernong leaves in the otherwise silent town square.

"What happened to them?" Otto asked quietly, though he could already guess at the answer.

"Their new neighbors were less than kind," the Vine said simply. "Nearly three hundred years ago, a creaking ship of settlers landed on the shore. They were already half starved when they arrived and barely prepared to survive here. They would have starved if the Secotan hadn't shown them where to find food and water and taught them how to plant crops in this soil. It was only with the Secotan's help that the settlers made it through the winter and built their Fort Roanoke."

"But for all the aid they were given, the settlers never liked the Secotan people. Their general accused the Secotan of stealing from him, but it was all pretense. A lie to justify what he and the rest of them had already made up their mind to do. They killed the Secotan chief and his men, burned down their houses, and chased any Secotan who was still alive off the island.

"I hope some of the survivors made a new home for themselves out there. But I never saw them again," the Vine said with a deep sadness.

"Then Fort Roanoke—the Lost Colony. They didn't disappear, did they?" Otto asked.

"Yes," the Vine said. "I ate them. I wasn't as strong back then, but I snatched every single one of them into the ground. When the next batch of settlers, your ancestors, came to the island, there wasn't anything left to find but the old fort. I promised from that day that I would keep the island safe. And I'll start by getting rid of these rotten intruders."

Screams broke out again. The scuppernong vines and plant corpses began to drag the hapless tourists toward their final destination once more.

"Otto!" Clancy called out. He was trying to grab a captured tourist, but the strength of the vines broke through his grasp easily.

Otto remained silent through the chaos, his mind racing. Between the newfound history of the Secotan and the fate of Fort Roanoke, he was not sure what he could even say to the Vine. It had read his true feelings so easily, and he knew that simple showmanship and flattery would not save anyone this time. Remembering the Vine's story, he pictured a scene of the scuppernong and the Secotan living peacefully on the island hundreds of years ago. A thought struck him at last.

"And that's all the more reason to let these people go!" he said.

"What?" the Vine asked in surprise.

"Yes, everything you said is true. What happened to the Secotans was not right, but their story will never live past the shores of this island if you eat these people now. This injustice will only continue if it stays buried in the ground, and what good does that do you or the Secotans? Instead, I have a proposal for you," Otto said with a gleam in this eye.

The Vine listened with interest.

The morning sun rose over Roanoke Island as the ferry propelled its way to shore. On the pier, lines of tourists were waiting to board. They were tired and scuffed from last night's misadventures, but alive and ready to return to the mainland. Among them was one particular farmhand: Ottavio "Otto" Hartcastle.

Thanks to his negotiations last night, the tourists were freed to return home and take with them the true tale of Roanoke. But there were two more conditions to the deal. First, that the Summer Harvest Festival would be redone to celebrate the island's complete history from here on. Given her prescient knowledge of the island, Lottie Baum had been chosen for the task. Second was that Otto would make his way west after all with a mission of his own.

The mayor had given him enough funds for a train ticket to Independence, Missouri. Lottie had even gifted him a new carpet bag that went fetchingly with his color waistcoat. In it were the few possessions he had: his shaving kit, his good changes of clothes, and a pouch full of scuppernong seeds. These he would take all the way to Oregon, making sure that everywhere he stopped, he found someone to plant them so they could grow into their own thriving grape vines one day.

The ferry's steam whistle blew just as Clancy came running up to him, canvas sack in tow.

"Otto! I finished packing and I'm ready to go," he said.

Otto took a deep breath and braced himself for a conversation he had been dreading. "Clance, my friend, this is where we have to part ways for now."

"What do ya mean?" Clancy asked, his usually cheery smile replaced with a worried frown.

"What the Vine said last night was right, Clancy. I always thought I had the most rotten luck to grow up here. And I spent so much time dreaming about living in a place where things happened, I never bothered to see what was happening under my own nose. But you're different, Clancy. You've got a full-placed devotion to farmwork and a complete contentment with island life. You love this place as much as anyone, and you wouldn't be happy living in a big city or out on the trail," Otto said while trying to keep his voice firmer than he felt.

"But I won't be happy if you're not here, neither!" Clancy protested. "What will I do without you?"

Otto clutched his friend on the shoulder. "Same as you always have. You watch over the place until I come back, won't you?"

"You'll come back?" Clancy asked.

"Of course," Otto said before Clancy grabbed him into a big bear hug, and Otto let himself be crushed by it for several long moments.

"Okay, you lummox, let me catch my ferry. And you know, Ms. Lottie will be running the festival now. And who do you think I suggested help her with all the planning when I spoke to her last night?"

Clancy stared at him in shock as the ferry blew its final call.

"So since you'll be spending so much time together, you two better have at least one conversation by the time I get back!" Otto said.

They said their last goodbyes before Otto walked up the boarding ramp, alone. They were still waving to each other as the ferry set off, until Clancy was too far out for Otto to see.

As the ocean water surrounded him and the full island came into view, Otto thought to himself for the first time in his life how beautiful it was. August winds were stretching across the coast. Their cool breeze was pushing waves of haint blue over the Roanoke Sound and into the swaying whispers of the creeping spike-rush. Above him, the seagulls and terns were bobbing in the summer sky, catching the updraft like a ballet of dancing kites. And Otto knew that over all of this, the scuppernong grape vines kept watch.

WILDMAN

GABRIEL PERAGINE

An ominous haze hung over the sleepy town of Marion, prophesying the arrival of a stranger. For days before his arrival, the town buzzed with wild rumors. In her typical gossipy fashion, Miss Martha whispered among the townsfolk that the man who had purchased the late Ol' John's land, was a devil-worshippin' Yank.

As the days passed, Martha's gossip took on a life of its own. Some folks claimed he was the son of a rich politician, others whispered he was a snake oil salesman, and a few insisted that he was the devil himself. Each outlandish rumor only fueled Milo's curiosity. It didn't matter which rumor was true; an outsider was a novelty here.

Milo and his sister Evelynn sat in their room, huddled over candlelight as Evelynn murmured her fantasies about the mystery man. Milo nodded along, only half-hearing her. It wasn't until a pillow smacked him in the face that he realized he had drifted off.

"Are you even listenin'? It's not every day we get a mysterious new suitor strollin' in."

Milo threw the pillow back with a grin. "I think Ma's right. Those romance novels are giving you sinful thoughts."

"At least I won't be an old maid! You've got one foot in the grave, at the ripe ol' age of twenny four."

Milo frowned. "You better hush before you wake Ma and Pa." He gave an exaggerated stretch as he leaned back on his bed. "I'm mighty tired anyway."

As the sun sagged in the sky the next day, a man drove a horse-drawn carriage in from the long road into town. The first house he passed by was nestled deep in the thicket of Mountain Laurel, tucked away from the rest of town. Miss Martha and her husband Joseph lived there, separate from everyone, much to everyone's relief. As soon as the sound of hoofbeats graced Miss Martha's ears, she tore down the dirt road to warn anyone who would listen that the devil had arrived in Marion.

"He's here! He's here! The devil's in Marion!"

She shouted it at the top of her lungs. Eyes averted their gaze, and slow walks became panicked scurries. Anyone with good sense knew not to lock eyes with Miss Martha lest they be pulled into one of her brimstone-fueled spells. Miss Martha knocked on every door she could. Most pretended they weren't home, and the unlucky few who answered the door made quick work of politely shooing her away.

The last house on the road sat next to a sea of tobacco plants. The sweet, earthy plant scent mixed with that of pine and meat wafting out from a chimney. It was quaint compared to the others in town, made of old oak and the sweat of Milo's great-grandpappy.

Martha's old, weathered voice interrupted Evelynn and Milo as they finished washing up the dishes from brunch. It wasn't the first time she'd appeared at their door shouting, but usually it was a form of proselytizing, not frenetic screaming. Evelynn gave a knowing glance at Milo, who returned a nod and a smug grin. Listening to the old woman's prattling would at least give them something interesting to talk about later.

When Evelynn opened the door, Milo saw Miss Martha's gray hair disheveled into a rat's nest, with wide eyes and needlepoint irises.

"Miss Martha, I thought Ma told you not to come around here. You're lucky she didn't hear you, or you'd be locking eyes with Pa's shotgun."

"That devil man is in town. And on a Sunday, to boot. I wouldn't be doing my duty as a godly woman if I didn't tell you."

A coy smile spread across Evelynn's face. "Ain't that somethin'? Well, where is that devil man? I'm in need of a good husband."

Miss Martha pursed her lips. "The devil ain't no laughin' matter. I saw a devil clear as day walkin' round my property just last night. And now Lucifer himself is a comin'. He's likely in the town center by now."

Evelynn peeked her head back into the kitchen to look at Milo.

"The mysterious suit–devil is in town, Milo."

Lifting his gaze from the dish he was pretending to wash, Milo said, "That so? I suppose we should go and see for ourselves."

Milo put the half-washed dish in the sink. "I'll get my shoes."

"We'll see you in town," Evelynn said, closing the door.

When Milo and Evelynn arrived in the town center, half the town was already there. They all waited, the girls for their suitor, the elders for a target to judge, and the gossips for new fodder.

Milo didn't imagine a devil or even a handsome suitor. Unlike Evelynn, he didn't fantasize about that sort of thing. His mind produced the image of an elderly aristocrat in sharp business attire riding in a fancy pants carriage. Neither vision held any truth.

Instead, a scrawny, bespectacled man emerged from the fog, hunched over his horse, drawing a plain wooden carriage. He looked to be about Milo's age, not an old aristocrat after all.

Evelynn scrunched up her nose and groaned, "Thought he'd be cuter."

Milo read Evelynn's expression like a book. The stranger clearly wasn't the prince Evelynn had been picturing, but none of the Marion boys were, either. She'd often complain to Milo about how the boys were either too rude, too dirty, or too dull. He didn't blame her too much. The romance books Evelynn devoured tainted her imagination with fantasies of fated loves and happy homemaking. The man of her dreams couldn't exist outside of book pages.

Milo didn't have those dreams. He couldn't imagine juggling children in tow while managing his wifely duties. Not that he didn't want a family—he did—but he couldn't quite picture it. Every time he tried to imagine his future, it was blank. But in a place like Marion, there was no other end, so he tried not to let his mind linger on it.

The stranger was different than anyone Milo had met, and that made him magnetic. The only world Milo knew was Marion. The only book he read was the Bible. The stranger brought with him something else, something forbidden. Milo felt a soft hunger that drew him in and called him to learn more.

The stranger yanked the reins, stopping in the middle of the circle of townsfolk that formed around him.

"Good evening. I wasn't expecting a welcoming party. Especially not on a Sunday afternoon."

The chatter amongst the group died down, and only the

chirping of crickets and croaks of frogs could be heard. An elderly man in a faded black cassock stepped out from the crowd.

"Welcome to Marion. I'm Preacher Thomas. You must be the one from New York. We're here to give you a proper southern welcome. It's not every day we get someone new."

"Dr. Simon Wil—"

Miss Martha's screeching pierced the air. "A preacher should know better than to invite the devil inside! No godly man travels on Sunday!"

The preacher gave an exasperated sigh. "Forgive her. She forgets her manners."

"Manners? Are you a false preacher?" Miss Martha railed. "Be sober, be vigilant; because your adversary the devil, as a roaring lion, walketh about, seeking whom he may devour."

The crowd edged away from her, as if Miss Martha's words carried with them a sickness. Her husband pushed himself through, grabbed her by the arm and yanked her away as she continued to shout. "Come, woman, you've embarrassed me enough for one night!"

Simon pursed his lips together. "My apologies, preacher. I'm exhausted from my travels. I'd like to turn in for the night."

With that, Simon snapped his reins again. The preacher waved. "See you next Sunday."

He never made it to church, which only fueled the flames of town gossip. Milo searched for him at every opportunity, but Simon eluded him. He rarely made it into town, even to buy goods. With Miss Martha's shouting and the side eyes from everyone else, Milo could hardly blame the man.

If given the choice, Milo would avoid town himself. If he had his way, he'd live deep in the woods like a hermit, away from the side glances and the gossip. Milo often ventured to the wooded areas behind his family's farm to enjoy solitude.

Amongst the sounds of trickling water and the tapping of woodpeckers, Milo felt like maybe he belonged there. The forest beckoned to him, and he often imagined himself fleeing into the dark wildness of it, never to return. He'd heard stories about people disappearing in it. He imagined they'd wandered in and been whisked away to somewhere better. Unlike the stories, Milo figured if he disappeared, his Ma and Pa would track him down and have him back before sundown.

As the sun set in the woods, Milo's mind drifted to better things. The weight of something hefty crashing on him snapped him to attention.

"Wh-"

Simon's eyes were dark pools so close to Milo that he could feel his eyelashes. He reared back and kicked his gangly legs around until he managed to get to his feet.

"Oh...uh, hello there. My apologies, I didn't think there would be anyone out here to witness my... clumsiness."

He dusted off his jacket and extended a hand. "I'm Simon Wilcott. Doctor Simon Wilcott."

Milo flopped his hand into Simon's for a limp-wristed shake. "Uh...Mildred." The sound of his words made his body tremble. Mildred was his god-given name. A perfectly acceptable girl's name, by all accounts, but one that never quite stuck with him. Everyone knew him as Mildred, but he knew he was Milo, even if they didn't.

As Milo's eyes refocused on Simon, he noticed how out of place the newcomer was. His sharp, tawny, two-piece suit was something he'd expect out of a businessman, not someone wandering through the forest.

Milo tugged at the hem of his dress, and his voice shrank to a meek whisper. "So, uh...what are you doing out here?"

Simon gazed off into the distance and began walking.

"Studies."

Milo followed behind him as he began to wander deeper into the forest. "What kind?"

Keeping his eyes forward, Simon stopped. His lips tightened for a moment before he muttered, "Nothing that would be of interest."

"I'm interested!"

"It's not the type of research the god-fearing type would appreciate."

A strange feeling wormed its way into Milo's chest. It wasn't the stuff of Evelynn's romance novels, but Simon's words held a magic power. Milo sputtered his words as he tossed the feeling around in his mind to determine its flavor.

"I...I mean...y-no..."

Simon's hand shot up to silence the conversation.

"I'm sure you're a lovely girl, but before you go on prattling about me joining your parish, I'd rather save us both the time."

Milo blinked in confusion, "Parish?" He gave a shallow chuckle. "I don't like being there much myself; I wouldn't subject you to that torture. I just wanted to know what you're studying. I could point you in the right direction. I know these woods like the back of my hand."

The sky uttered a soft rumble before trickling water on their heads. It grumbled louder and louder, and then roared as it dumped buckets on the forest below.

"Not now though...or we might get drowned."

Simon's scowl melted into a half-smile. "I see. Well, we can continue this conversation later. You're more than welcome to stop by my home. I'm usually there in the afternoon. I could use a hand in unpacking if you're willing."

Milo spoke barely above a whisper. "I'd love to."

With a final nod, Simon departed for the real world, leaving Milo frozen in the wilderness alone. For the first time since he could remember, the solitude felt lonely.

Milo barely made it home in time for dinner. Neither of his parents noticed his absence, or his soaked dress. Evelynn was another matter. She immediately noticed the uncharacteristic lightness in his steps. Staring at him unapologetically, Evelynn's eyes darted from side to side to signal that she knew something was up and wanted to discuss it. Milo shoveled food into his mouth without acknowledgment. Once they excused themselves, they gabbed about Milo's meeting with Simon.

Of course, Evelyn began cooking up theories about their future together and how Simon might be the one to change Milo into something more palatable, something more wife-shaped.

Evelynn meant well, but the conversation left a bitter taste in Milo's mouth. Evelynn was more than palatable; people liked her, and they had an implicit understanding of her. Judgmental looks never so much as grazed her.

Milo was a different case. He and everyone else knew it. They knew it before he could conceptualize what "it" was. His mother was probably the first to recognize it. Like a blacksmith molding a piece of iron, she'd tried to hammer Milo's soul into her desired shape. But all of the bruises, cuts, and broken bones in the world had just made him retreat deeper within himself.

"You don't have to get so pouty about it," Evelynn prodded.

"It's not about that."

Evelynn leaned back on the bed, exasperated from trying to understand. "You know Ma will kill you if she finds you've been sneaking out to a man's house, right? Especially him. 'Sides, you don't know what kind of fella he is. He could really be the devil."

Milo smirked. "Could be. But I think that's why I like him."

"Only a devil could tame you, Mildred."

Milo deflated. "You gotta help me see him. Ma can't know."

Evelynn gave Milo a long, sideways glance. "Fine."

She shifted on the bed, straightening herself. "But only if I get all your dessert for the next month. It's my final offer."

Milo hopped off the bed, "Thanks, Eve."

The next day, the two conspired to get Milo to Simon's house. Milo only had a few hours while his mother and sister were preoccupied with tending to farm animals, but that's all he figured he needed. As soon as Evelynn gave the go-ahead, Milo sprinted to Simon's house as fast as his legs would allow.

Half out of breath, he arrived and rapped on Simon's door. There was the sound of shuffling, followed by a long pause, then the sound of locks being unbound.

Waving Milo inside, Simon bowed gently. "My apologies, I had to make sure you weren't Father Thomas."

Milo's whole being was flooded with a sense of awe. Ol' Man John's former home was lavish by Marion's standards, with long glass windows, ornately decorated banisters, and a balcony. The interior was dusty, yet held a refined charm. Scattered around the house were boxes and crates filled with all sorts of unusual knick-knacks, small machines, and piles on piles of books. If he hadn't already known this was someone's house, Milo would have mistaken it for a library or a museum.

"You weren't kidding about the unpacking..." Milo mused.

"I'm a bit of a pack rat. Come, I'll put on some tea, and we can chat before we get to work."

Simon handed Milo a steaming cup of fragrant, floral-smelling tea. "So, you're interested in my studies."

Milo gently blew on his tea as he nodded. Simon sat in the chair across from him and said in a serious tone, "What do you know about the Wildman?"

There was a pause before Milo looked up from his teacup. "The old wives' tale? I've heard of it."

"Seen anything?"

"No."

"What can you tell me about it?"

Milo stirred his tea nervously. "Not much, I suppose. There's been stories passed down about it for generations. They say it's what takes folks that go too far yonder into the holler. As kids, they used to tell us that if you did something God would be ashamed of, the Wildman would grab you up." Milo slapped his knee and chuckled.

Quirking an eyebrow, Simon leaned in. "So you don't believe in it?"

"Not especially. Pa said he saw it one time huntin' for bucks. Said it was just a sick grizzly."

Simon's neutral expression began to sag into a frown. The disappointment was palpable.

"Is that what you're studying? The Wildman?"

Simon grabbed a pile of books off the side table and plopped them down onto the table between them. "I study the occult. The Wildman is one of many subjects I intend to study. I needed a quiet place to start, and Marion fit the bill."

A hearty laugh burst out of Milo. "Marion?"

Pink spread across Simon's visage.

"I admit I didn't do my due diligence before arriving. I thought I'd get some peace here, but I underestimated the power of nosy church gossips."

Milo smiled. For the first time in a while, he felt a sense of camaraderie with someone in this town. He kept asking question after question, absorbing each thing Simon said. It was mainly monologues, but Milo was still enamored. It wasn't Simon's words that drew him, but his conviction in them. It wasn't the fiery passion of Father Thomas or any other preacher. Simon's voice was low and melodic, with a magic that soothed Milo to his core.

They never did get to unpacking. By the time the clock tolled, it had already been nearly three hours. Milo scurried home as fast as he could. Luckily, his parents hadn't detected him missing, and as soon as he arrived, he was already scheming ways to visit Simon again.

Milo found every excuse he could think of to go to town and visit Simon. It wasn't long until his mother found out. His body reflexively tensed up, anticipating the usual tirade about honoring godliness. Her mouth opened wide, poised to unleash holy hellfire, but nothing came out. It was silent. Painfully silent, until she grumbled to herself, "At least she's starting to act like a woman."

Milo's stomach twisted into knots, settling into a deep, heavy shame. The yelling would've been easier. His mother's insistence on him playing the role of a wife and eventually a mother hurt him more. The girl in her mind wasn't him; she was just a trick of the light, a fleeting dream that his mother imagined. His mother would never accept the truth of things, nor would anyone else in Marion.

From that day on, his mother only spoke in sideways glances. Milo knew she believed Simon was his suitor. Even an ungodly man was better than none. Day after day, Milo ran to Simon's. He'd share more about Marion, helping Simon map out new places to hunt for the Wildman. Sometimes, they'd go into the woods and wander around. Every tree and hill was familiar, but Simon's presence gave it a spark. They never discovered much, only fragments of old farm equipment, buried arrowheads, oddly stacked animal bones, and the remains of old fire pits.

Simon wanted to scope out the area at night, hoping there'd be more of a chance of finding the being. All the reports of the Wildman had been at night. Simon mused that the creature was nocturnal. There were more dangerous things out in the woods after dark, like cougars or wolves. The two agreed to wait to camp out until they determined the most suitable area.

On their excursions, they had ample time to chat. Simon spoke about a wide range of things. He told Milo about his dream to understand all the world's secrets. He talked about his studies, the history of ancient Greece, the mathematics of planets' orbits, and the cultures of people Milo would never speak to.

When they were alone, Milo dropped his pretenses. He began to share pieces of himself–his dreams, his disconnectedness from the rest of Marion, and even the tumultuous relationship with his mother. Simon met every new thought Milo shared with understanding and reassurance. It was so different from what he knew that it stirred something deep within him.

He began to imagine futures for himself, sometimes as a farmhand, sometimes as a man of science like Simon, and sometimes even as a world traveler. The fantasies were never the same, but there was one thing they had in common. He wasn't Mildred. He was a man named Milo.

Anyone with eyes could see it, despite his best efforts to hide it. He had watched the girls in town to mimic the way their hips swayed and the cadence of their speech. Despite his best efforts, every move was awkward and stilted–a collection of disparate parts fighting against one another rather than a fully formed person.

The noise that thing created in his head grew and grew. With each passing day, it occupied more of his mind. Eventually, the noise became too loud for Milo to ignore. It was not enough that the image existed in the confines of his mind; it needed out.

He mulled over the idea of what to do with it. Later that week, he was left at home alone while family ventured into town for groceries. Even without their presence, he was careful to step on the floorboards so they wouldn't creak. They might not be able to hear him, but God could. Milo hoped if he was quiet enough, maybe even God couldn't see him.

Once he got into Pa's room, he stood there for several minutes, eyeing the dresser. Something called out to him to just do it, but his mind told him that he shouldn't. The last time he was here, he was only knee high. He'd played house with Evelynn only hours earlier, and was deep in the fantasy of being a cowboy—one where he was big and strong like his Pa, a fearless hero and hunter. Tiny hands riffled through Pa's drawers to find the perfect costume. It was only a minute or two before Pa found him. He didn't say a word to Milo. He just silently brought Ma into the room. With one swift beating, Milo's fantasies, innocence, and view of his Pa were shattered.

Still, the beckoning now was stronger than the time-worn memory or his reason. Milo tied up his hair in a braid and sat it atop his head in a frizzy nest of blonde hair. He plopped one of Pa's hats on top. He threw on an oversized button-up and ratty pair of slacks he recovered from the dresser and paraded his new look in front of his mirror. He couldn't believe how much lighter and how much more himself he felt. Just the mismatched outfit brought Milo joy that he had never known as Mildred.

The rattling of the doorknob brought Milo's fantasy crashing down around him. They weren't supposed to be back yet. He rushed to pull off the clothes, but it was too late. His mother's gaze met his, and a white-hot rage exploded within her.

There was no exchange of words. Only an inhuman, unintelligible screech, followed by Milo's hat being ripped off and Ma snatching his braid. He writhed, trying to break himself free, but Ma's grip was as tight as a bulldog's bite.

Milo kicked and screamed, but no one other than Evelynn

or Pa would hear him. Neither of them would intervene, lest they be on the receiving end of Ma's wrath. Ma didn't bother to grab a switch this time. She grabbed anything else she could get ahold of: a candlestick, a rolling pin, and a poker from the fireplace, using each until she got bored of it. The poker, still warm from that day's fire, sizzled as it touched his skin, causing Milo to yelp.

There was no mercy, no attempt at forging him into something else. Each strike to Milo's body was given with the intent to destroy him completely.

After it was all done, Milo lay bloodied and black and blue on the floor. His brain registered pain, but he was so detached from himself that he couldn't feel it. It took a moment, and then the tears poured out all at once.

"Mildred?"

Evelynn peered around the door. As she saw him, her face drained of all color and she collapsed to her knees. Evelynn touched his face as if it were broken glass.

"Mildred...are you...?"

Sticky wet drops fell onto Milo's shoulder. The tightness of her embrace gave Milo a painful reminder of his injuries. He flinched, and Evelynn withdrew.

"I'm fine...nothin's broken."

"I love you Mildred, but...can't you... for your own sake...?"

She didn't say it directly, but she didn't have to. Evelynn knew what he was, and she knew how Ma felt about it.

Running his hand across his face, he wiped off the blood. "No."

"I think I saw some mice in the kitchen. Better show Ma and Pa before they get into the pantry again."

Evelynn left. Between her words was a plea for him to be safe. He knew what must be done.

He couldn't stay here, not anymore. He fled into the rainy

night and to Simon's. His eyes stung with shame and anger. Hot tears mixed with the icy rain gushed down his face.

He stood in Simon's doorway, shivering and soaked through in the cold rain. Anxiety seized him every time he tried to knock, locking his body as if rigor mortis had set in.

Would Simon understand? Would going home be better? Was it even worth saying anything, or was it best that he disappear into the woods?

He squeezed his eyes tightly to shut the racing thoughts out, and a flurry of knocks exploded out of him. As soon as Simon opened the door, Milo collapsed in his arms, shivering from exhaustion and cold rain. Simon stiffened. He awkwardly tried to wrap his arms around Milo in an approximation of a hug.

"Are you...okay?" Simon asked in quiet trepidation.

Milo sniffled, trying to get a breath in.

"I-I..."

"Come, I have some tea on the fire," Simon said, ushering Milo in.

Milo sniffled faintly as they sat together in the reading room. The candlelight cast Milo's wounds in shadow, revealing welts and bruises. Simon crouched in front of him and gently brushed Milo's blonde locks from his face, then shuddered as he beheld the results of Ma's handiwork.

"Let me get you a cold rag."

Simon scurried off to the kitchen and brought back a cold cloth. Pressing it lightly against Milo's face, his usual matter-of-fact voice morphed into something more tender.

"You should hold it there until the swelling goes down. That mother of yours has a fury I imagine even the devil himself couldn't rival."

Milo stifled a laugh. "She'd give the devil a run for his money."

"And what did you do to incur the she devil's wrath this time?"

Milo's smile disappeared, and he hung his head low, muttering, "Same thing it always is. I'm not...right."

Simon firmly placed a hand on Milo's shoulder, and with the other, he pushed Milo's chin up. Their eyes met–Milo's blues contained within them an unexplored ocean of sorrow. "You look right to me, save for the marks of your mother's lashings. That's what's not right. *You* are just fine."

A swell of emotions caught in Milo's throat as he tried to force them down. His thoughts tripped over themselves, sputtering to a near stop.

"I..I..." and then the words Milo never meant to utter slid out of his mouth. "I'm not a girl!"

Milo reflexively tensed up, ready for the impact of another lashing or, even worse, jeering. He fought his urge to shield his face from whatever incoming attack would be thrown at him.

But it never came. Simon stared at him, not saying a word. His gaze was different from the others'. There was no disgust or malice behind it–only the quiet curiosity he had every time he opened a new book or made a new discovery in the woods.

Simon broke the silence. "If not a girl, then what?"

The gears in Milo's brain stopped turning. Out of all the outcomes he had imagined, this wasn't among them.

"Uh...well...a man, I guess."

Simon blinked in confusion. "But why?"

Milo exhaled sharply. "I don't know. Maybe the good Lord messed up along the way. Maybe I'm haunted by demons. Maybe I'm cursed. I don't know. And I don't care." He paused before mumbling, "Not everything needs an answer."

Simon rapidly blinked. The idea of not wanting to know must be foreign to him. The scholar wanted to know every answer, regardless of how big or small it was, and this was an interesting question.

"If anyone would have the answer, it would be you. How did you get to this conclusion?"

"Does it matter? It's how I feel. How I've always felt."

Simon paused for a moment. "In practice, I suppose not."

Then he huffed like a child denied dessert before whipping around to collect the empty teacups.

"What will you do, then? I can't imagine your parents are too pleased with this."

Milo sank into his chair, thinking about the possibilities, but couldn't come up with anything other than becoming an old witch in the forest.

"I don't know. I can't stay, but I don't know where I'd go."

Simon paced back and forth, brow furrowed in thought. "As far as you can from here. A different state, at least."

Marion, as horrible as it was, was what Milo knew. He couldn't think of anywhere else. Beyond Simon's stories, he knew nothing of the world outside.

"New York?" Milo mused.

Simon shook his head. "It's better than Marion, but it's a different beast." He held up a finger, "One moment, I have an idea."

Simon bolted out of the room. Clattering teacups and the rustling of papers could be heard before Simon returned from the kitchen and slammed a crinkled map on the table in front of them. The map was creased, tattered, and brown with old age. Across it were various Xs drawn crudely in red ink.

"The Wildman is just one story I planned to investigate." Simon pointed to one of the red Xs in Louisiana. "Each of these is a place I planned to visit eventually. There were enough places in spitting distance from Marion, so I settled here. But...

it hasn't been what I expected. I think I'd like to explore the new frontier out west. You can come with me."

Milo paused. He'd never considered the West, but it was more appealing than New York. He wasn't a city boy by any means, and the new frontier could provide him with a familiar place to settle.

Milo grinned. "Out west it is. But only on one condition..."

Taking a big breath in, he swallowed his fear. "I get to be Milo." Exhilaration and panic filled his body as soon as he uttered the name. Milo felt good, but it was tempered by the guilt he felt for speaking it aloud. He glanced at Simon, searching for any hint of what he felt. Simon remained stone-faced before nodding.

"Okay. Milo, it is."

Relief washed over Milo. Just like that, the moment he both feared and anticipated was over.

"Before we leave, there is one thing I'd like to do," Simon added. "We have checked most of the area for the Wildman. The only place left is that little sliver of woods east. We can hit it on our way out."

Milo bit the inside of his cheek to keep himself from groaning.

"You sure? That's near Miss Martha's farm. I don't think either of us wants to run into her."

Simon waved off the concern. "We won't stay too long. We'll be out before sunrise."

Neither of them slept that night. Their minds were wide awake with the thoughts of adventure. They spent hours packing, cramming as many books and supplies as they could fit in the wagon.

After all the supplies were gathered, Simon allowed Milo to pick through his closet. Milo was almost overwhelmed with the options. The clothes hung off his frame, making him seem frail and boyish, but that didn't matter. To him, they were better than the world's most flattering gown. He took some old fabric scraps and wrapped them around his chest. The orbs of flesh he had come to hate were flattened into something more uniform. It wasn't perfect, but it was close. There was just one last thing to take care of.

Milo grabbed a pair of kitchen scissors from the pantry. His hands shook as he raised the scissors to his head. He'd never cut his hair, not in his entire life. Cutting it now felt more final than everything else. It was a full step away from here and into himself, like stepping off a cliff into a dark unknown.

Simon, arms full of boxes, glanced over. "Do you need help? I'm no barber, but I can guarantee it will be shorter."

Milo nodded silently and handed Simon the scissors.

With one swipe, Milo's waist-length hair was now a short bob near his ears. He opened his eyes and smiled back at his reflection in the mirror. A wave of euphoria washed over him as he beheld his own countenance. Never had he imagined that he could see himself as he truly was.

There weren't many good things in Milo's life, so when one hobbled its way to him, he couldn't help but ask why.

"Back when we first met, what made you invite me over?"

Simon stopped cutting. "You seemed curious, and I'm a teacher."

Milo deflated. He wasn't sure what answer he'd wanted, but it wasn't that one.

Sinking down into his chair, he asked, "Is that the only reason?"

"No. You seemed a bit...peculiar. Not in a bad way, just different than all the others here. As a peculiar person, I find myself drawn to other peculiar people."

It wasn't clear what it was about Simon's words that soothed him so, but Milo's shoulders untensed immediately, and he sank farther back into the chair as Simon continued cutting his hair. The cuts weren't clean, but they were enough.

They both agreed it would be better to leave before sunrise. Milo's Ma and Pa wouldn't look for them once they had gone, but staying too long would risk confrontation. Still, there was one person in Marion who would miss him: Evelynn.

The two fought about whether or not to visit her, but Milo's steadfastness won out. They quietly drove the wagon toward Milo's old home through the rain that was now a torrential downpour. With quiet feet and a lantern, Milo tiptoed to Evelynn's window and lightly knocked. After the third knock, Evelynn shuffled about in the darkness, searching for the source of the noise.

She turned and faced the window, gasping as she beheld the silhouette of a boyish figure. She gasped, and before she could let out a shout, Milo hissed, "Eve! Shhh! It's me!"

She rushed to open the window.

Squinting her eyes to try to make out Milo, Eve whispered, "Mildred..? I thought you were a man at my window! What are you doing? You shouldn't be back here. Ma might..."

Milo brushed Evelynn's hand off his face. "It's fine. I just wanted to stop here and say...."

Evelynn paused, then drew in a long breath. "To say goodbye?"

Milo's mouth trembled as he softly said, "Yes...but I'll write you one day. I'll send you letters. From Milo."

Evelynn nearly fell out of the window as she embraced Milo. He felt the hot stickiness as her tears dripped on his shirt. Milo worried Evelynn might tear a hole in his shirt as she whiteknuckled it, but it was to be expected. Evelynn needed to store this moment away and use it for the lifetime she'd have without him. After a moment that seemed to last eons, Evelynn released him. "You'd better get going before the roosters start crowing." Milo vanished into the night, engulfed in the darkness where no watchful eyes would follow him.

Milo gripped the leather reins, gently guiding the wagon softly through the woods. Simon was beside him, squinting to read the map in the pre-dawn gloam.

"I know where we're going," Milo said, tugging the reins.

Simon folded the map and tucked it into his breast pocket. "I'll keep a watch then."

The two sat in silence as they trotted deeper and deeper into the tangled mass of trees. The sky gave a deep grumble before a flash of lightning cracked across the sky. In that brief moment of light, Milo saw the figure of something that looked vaguely human. Its gait was lumbering, and it bent forward with a wide stance. It put one foot in front of the other, just like a man but the rest of it felt uncanny.

"Simon! Simon! I think I saw it!" Milo shouted, pointing into the forest. He jerked the reins back to turn the horse around in pursuit.

The dark shadow darted across the side of the trail, too fast for either of them to catch a proper glimpse. Milo snapped the reins again, propelling the stallion even faster into the woods. But it was too late. Whatever it was had already disappeared.

Halting the carriage, Milo murmured, "I know I saw something..."

Simon was already halfway off the carriage. "Maybe it left some clues."

Milo hopped off to join Simon and tied the horse to a nearby tree.

"If the rain hasn't washed it away," Milo said as he took a lantern and examined the air around him. The rain stung his eyes, making his already murky night vision even murkier. The nearby stream was rushing, engorged from days of heavy rain. No other sound could be heard. Not the owls, nor the crickets. Milo couldn't remember the last time the woods had been so devoid of life.

Swinging his lantern around, Milo's eyes caught a glint of something red.

"Over here!"

The ground swished under their feet and their boots sank into the wet peat. The light revealed a scramble of red mush next to a pile of bones organized in a perfect circle. In the middle of them, there was charred wood, small pieces of torn fabric, and eating utensils. Milo recoiled. The odor of death and spoiled meat wafted from the mush pile.

Simon turned to Milo. "What kind of animal does something like that?"

"Not one I know of. Cougars and bears don't usually leave bones like that."

At that moment a surge of water rushed through them, submerging their ankles. The stream had overflowed into a growing river. The horse bucked and whinnied as the water swelled.

"We gotta move now or we'll be washed out!" Milo hollered.

The two sprinted toward the carriage, and Milo fumbled to untie the horse from the tree. The water rose from the hem of his pants to his ankles. He finally managed to untangle the reins and shouted, "Go!" Milo and Simon leaped into the carriage.

Hooves struggled to get their grip on the ground as it began washing away. Milo steered the horse through the thicket, thorns catching skin and clothing. Simon tucked his head beneath his arms to protect himself. Milo didn't flinch; he ignored the scrapes and pricks. Their sting was only a nuisance compared to his mother's rage.

Finally, they made it up to a clearing in the trees. In the center was a cabin that looked like it hadn't been used in decades. The roof drooped, heavy with moss and debris, and the chimney lazily leaned against an old evergreen. An unsettling aura hung around the otherwise unremarkable cabin.

In the distance, Milo saw structures littered across the clearing. At first glance, they looked like people. He elbowed Simon. "What is that?"

Simon rubbed the rain off his glasses and put them back on. "Don't know. They're too still to be anything animate."

As they drew closer, the amber glow of the lamps revealed several crosses sprinkled about the clearing, tied together with twine. Some of them had tufts of hay arranged into humanoid shapes splayed across the wood in crude crucifixions.

When they grew closer, the sound of clanking glass was all around them. Milo looked up and noticed light reflecting off jars hanging from the nearby trees. He wasn't sure what the jars were for, but their presence caused a pit of dread to form in his stomach.

Another crack of lightning lit up the sky. The horse reared up, and Milo used all his force to try to keep it steady. Once the horse settled down, he leaned in to stroke its mane. As he shifted his weight forward, his eyes met a black figure in the distance. Its eyes let out a soft red glow, and it had the bat-like wings of what could only be a devil. Milo recoiled, but before he could say a word, the flash of lightning nearly blinded him. When his eyes focused again, the figure was gone.

Milo was frozen in fear. Simon shouted at him, snapping him back to reality,

"Milo! Shelter!"

They raced to the cabin. The closer they got, the more

Milo's soul squirmed and screamed for him to run away. He leaned toward Simon, his voice barely a whisper. "I saw something out there."

"The Wildman?!" Simon perked up.

"I don't think so...it had wings. And glowing red eyes."

"A different creature, then?" Simon shifted back and forth as he pondered the idea, before resigning himself. "We don't have enough time. Best not to get distracted."

Milo tied up the horse to a fence post, and they approached the cabin door. Simon jiggled the doorknob, but it was locked.

"Are you sure no one lives here?"

"This is Miss Martha's property, but this isn't her hous–"

At that moment, the door swung open, startling Milo. When he turned to face the doorway, he was met with the visage of something worse than any forest demon–Miss Martha. Her gray hair was tangled into a rat's nest with small tufts sticking out at varying angles. The thin, white lace nightgown made her look like some sort of ghastly spirit. In her hand, a small lamp cast shadows upward from beneath her chin, creating a harshness with the angles of her face.

"Mr. Wilcott, is it? What are you doing here at this unholy hour? And who is this?"

Milo lowered his head. His heart quickened. What if they recognized him? What if they notified his mother or the law?

Simon gave a gentle bow. "My apologies. We were traveling and got caught in the storm. We just needed some shelter for the night. We thought this cabin was abandoned." He gestured to Milo. "This is my research assistant, Milo."

The haggard voice of an old man called out from the cabin. "Who's at the door?"

Miss Martha called back, "Mr. Wilcott and his assistant."

Joseph appeared at the door, sleep still in his eyes, and a

rifle slung over one shoulder. He wiped his hands on his shirt and extended his hand toward Simon.

"My apologies, Doctor. Seeing as you've never been to church, I don't think I've ever introduced myself proper. I'm Joseph."

Simon pressed his lips together. He hesitantly placed his hand in Joseph's for a half-hearted shake. "Simon, Dr. Simon Wilcott. It's a pleasure."

Joseph turned to Milo, who let out an unconvincingly deep voice. "Nice to meet you..."

Miss Martha gave a warm grin. "We got flooded out, so we're staying the night here. We have a spare bedroom for you and the...boy."

The last word lingered with its lack of conviction. Milo wasn't sure whether he felt more comforted or afraid of it.

Simon's gaze met his for a moment before he turned back toward the couple. "We wouldn't want to impose on you. I'm sure we can find someplace to camp for the night."

Joseph's inviting tone soured into pointed, as he gripped his rifle. "That would be mighty rude of you. Coming onto our property, trying to enter our cabin, and then rejecting our grace. Folks in town wouldn't be too appreciative of that."

Milo suppressed a shudder. Simon bowed his head slightly. "Thank you for your hospitality. We'll try not to be too much trouble."

Once inside, things weren't much better. The fireplace in the center of the room bathed the interior with warm light. Dozens of hand-carved wooden crosses and small Mary figurines lined the walls. Their faces were turned toward them, unblinking, with the light cast below them giving their expressions an ominous air of judgment.

Milo's eyes darted around, searching for all the points of

escape. Instead, his gaze met that of the figures. Every fiber of him wanted to pick up and run, but he knew he couldn't.

"I need to tie up Lucian proper and grab some things from the buggy," Milo said as he inched toward. the door.

Joseph pointed. "There's a post just 'round the back."

Once outside, Milo could finally breathe again. The feeling of rain droplets on his skin soothed him with their tacit reminder that he was still alive.

He took Lucian by the reins and walked slowly as if he were wading through molasses. He stroked the horse softly as he spoke.

"Wish we could swap places. I think I'd be better off in the rain." Lucian gave a soft grunt of acknowledgement, then Milo rummaged through the back for dry clothes, tucked them under his jacket, and began walking back.

Something resembling a too-big man lumbered through the trees. As soon as Milo caught a glimpse of it, it stopped. The yellow-green reflection of its eyes flickered toward Milo and for a moment, they locked gazes.

Snap. Snap. Snap.

Branches and twigs broke in quick succession as the being began sprinting toward Milo, its gangly, ape-like limbs flailing about. Milo forgot all about the oddities of the cabin as a new fear overtook him. Before he knew what he was doing, he had already started sprinting back to the cabin. With a slam of the cabin door, he blocked out one horror for another.

Miss Martha, Simon, and Joseph, all seated in front of the fire, turned to face Milo in unison. Milo's chest heaved up and down in quick, shallow breaths, and the entirety of his body shook.

"Poor thing! You must be soaked to the bone!" Miss Martha said as she got up and put a hand on his shoulder, lightly rubbing it. The hairs on Milo's back stood on end. With each touch, Miss Martha made him want to jump straight out of his skin. She grabbed his face to turn it toward herself. "Don't worry sweetpea, we'll make sure you're taken care of."

A flicker of recognition flashed across Miss Martha's countenance. She squinted and leaned forward to try to get a clearer look. Milo leaned back in equal measure, turning his face away from the firelight.

"...you wouldn't be related to the Palmers, would you?"

Simon, seeing Milo squirm, interjected, "No, he's my cousin."

"...He?" Martha drew back in surprise, looking Milo up and down.

Milo, searching for a lifeline, spat out, "There's something...something out there...it walked like a man, but..."

Simon stood up. "What did it look like?"

"Yellow eyes, maybe seven...no...eight feet tall. Long arms."

Miss Martha guided Milo to a seat by the fire. "Good thing you came in, then. That devil would've eaten you whole."

Simon leaned in closer to Miss Martha. "You've seen the Wildman?"

"I've seen the shadow of the devil once or twice," Miss Martha said. "Whatever is in these woods has been causin' us a bit of trouble. Chickens, cows, and sheep go missin', along with some passersby."

Joseph clutched his rifle tightly. "I ain't never seen the thing. If I had, it'd be dead as a doornail by now. 'Nough of that talk. It's about time to turn in."

Raising a fist, Miss Martha scolded Joseph. "I saw what I saw. The devil doesn't come by here because the Lord protects us. He hasn't been close since I put the crosses up."

Joseph took a long drag of his pipe. "It's too late for your ramblings, woman. Make yourself useful and show them to bed."

Miss Martha dusted off her dress and gestured into the hallway.

"Your room is this way. It's a little dusty but likely a tad more comfy than a tent." Miss Martha directed them to the door in front of them. The inside of the room was cramped, with two little straw pallets thrown haphazardly onto crudely carved wooden bedframes.

There was no window here, just the stale stench of rotting wood and old straw. Miss Martha and Joseph were standing in the doorway, the only avenue out.

Joseph pulled out a pipe and took out a long drag, before turning to leave. "I think it's best we turn in for the night." He puffed out a large cloud of smoke as he locked eyes with Milo. "Good night. And remember, God don't take too kindly to liars."

With that, the couple shut the door and left. Milo let out a long breath of relief and fell back onto the straw bed. In the smallest voice he could muster, he whispered, "Simon...we got to get out of here."

Simon took off his jacket and casually sat on his bed. "I know. Believe me, I'm not thrilled either, but I think this was the best option. Just try to get some sleep. We'll be out first thing in the morning."

Tossing and turning, Milo tried for what felt like hours to get comfortable. Once the adrenaline left him, he was left with pain settling into his ribs. It felt like his bandages were about to cave in his chest and shatter the bones around it.

He stood up and wandered to the corner of the room. There was still light coming in from the crack in the door, but it was dark enough he felt like no eyes could see him.

He unbuttoned his shirt and slowly unraveled the fabric from around his chest, exposing it to the prickling of the icy mountain air.

Screeeee!

The otherworldly howl shattered the silence, shaking the trees and sending a flurry of flapping wings into the night.

Milo froze, unsure whether or not to cover himself or flee into the woods. Before he could process anything else, lamp-light flooded into the room. Milo whipped around and met a pair of eyes behind him–Miss Martha's eyes.

He tried his best to cover, but it was too late. She had already seen him. Miss Martha lunged at him, shrieking like a banshee as she clawed at Milo's chest. The grabbing hands weren't what frightened him. It was the thought of being Mildred that made his blood run cold.

Miss Martha's shrill cries pierced the air. Milo could hear Simon bumping in his half awake-half asleep haze. Simon clumsily reached around Miss Martha to restrain her. From his grunts, Milo could tell that he was using all of his strength to just keep her still. But she kept screaming and clawing at Milo.

Bang! The sound of a gunshot shook the entire cabin.

All heads turned to Joseph, who was looming in the doorway.

"She's a demon!" Miss Martha squealed, pointing at the bandages around Milo's chest.

Another howl reverberated through the cabin, this time even louder than before. Joseph glared at Milo and Simon, the bloodlust in his eyes obscuring any shimmer of humanity.

"What did I tell you folk about lying? Now look and see what you've done. You've brought the devil here!"

Milo wanted to yell back and scream and fight, but he was paralyzed.

"Let go of 'er" Joseph ordered, pointing the gun directly at Simon. Simon slowly loosened his grip.

"We don't want any troub-"

"I knew I recognized you... Mildred." Miss Martha spat his name.

The name rattled something in Milo's brain, and he lost all sense of preservation. Hurling himself at Miss Martha, he tackled her onto the bed and began swinging.

Simon, sensing Joseph lift his rifle, grabbed the middle of the barrel and attempted to yank it free from him.

GRRAAAAAAAR!

Another shriek thundered throughout the cabin; this time, the sound came within. Everyone froze. The thump of heavy footsteps on the old creaky floorboards, followed by the sliding of something heavy, echoed through the cabin..

Joseph turned to face the middle room. Illuminated by the lamplight was a human-like being, its hair black and matted, teeth thick and yellow, and dragging behind it the bloody hindquarters of a cow. It turned its snout upward, and its nostrils flared out as it sucked the stale cabin air in.

Joseph's hands shook violently as he aimed with his rifle.

"Back to hell!"

Bang!

It missed.

Bang!

It missed again.

Before Joseph could shoot a third time, the monster dropped the cow and galloped towards him on all fours like a rabid ape. It knocked him over, then banged wildly with its fists on Joseph's head until it was a pile of mush. Red sludge slid down the monster's forearms as he lifted his head up. It paused for a moment. Milo swore he saw it sneer at Joseph before it picked his limp body back up and ripped it apart like a bag of flour. Innards sloshed out of Joseph and splatted onto the floor. It then took Joseph's head, unhinged its jaw, and crunched an exposed part of his spine in its maw.

There was only silence from the three as they watched in abject horror at Joseph's dismemberment. Miss Martha, seizing a moment of opportunity, shoved Milo off, then grabbed him by the hair and yanked him to his feet, throwing him toward the monster.

"Here! Take her! She's the one you want! Take this sinner to hell with you!"

Milo stumbled into the monster, but it didn't acknowledge him. Instead, its eyes were fixated on Miss Martha. It cocked its head to the side as it lumbered forward. Miss Martha clutched the cross around her neck and lifted it up.

"In the name of Jesus, I rebuke you!"

It snarled, then flung itself full force at Miss Martha. She screamed and flailed wildly. The crunch of bone and the sloshing of viscera could be heard as the monster tore her limb from limb, followed by wet chomping as it tore flesh from bone.

Simon clambered to Milo and wrapped him tightly.

Simon's voice wobbled. "Leave us be. Please..."

The Wildman snorted as it tore Milo from Simon's grip. Simon stumbled backward into the wall, leaving Milo exposed. The Wildman's shadow loomed over him as he moved closer. The beast then slowly knelt down to Milo's level. Bits of flesh were wedged in between the creature's teeth and the smell of blood wafted from its mouth. It pressed its face against the top of Milo's head and took a deep whiff. It withdrew, blinking slowly.

The monster reached out his hand. Milo shut his eyes tightly waiting for his soul to be cast into hell. The pain never came, only the soft touch of something upon his head. He unclenched his eyes and met the Wildman's gaze. Its yellow eyes held a sweet almost puppy-dog feeling to them. Fingers trembling, Milo reached out and placed his hand on the beast's head. He gave gentle pets, causing the Wildman to let out a soft trill. It pointed at Milo then to itself.

Milo couldn't put into words what the monster was communicating, but he understood it. Milo mirrored its gesture back to it. The monster stood back up, grunted, then walked away.

Both were speechless, unsure of how to process what had just happened. Milo stood up, shook straw and blood off of him, and buttoned his shirt back up, "We need to get out of here."

Purple and orange splotches began appearing in the sky as the sun rose. The morning light filtered through the cabin, revealing Simon's bewildered expression.

Simon mumbled, "What...was that...thing?"

Milo looked at him and smiled, "Something peculiar."

"Yes, quite. But why did it...?"

Milo shrugged, "Dunno. But maybe we're not supposed to."

BURIED: A CRYPTID (LOVE?) STORY

ANTONIO DINKENS

I don't think I knew what it meant to be in love as a kid. I didn't recognize it in the way I always wanted to play with him. How when I saw something interesting, I always wanted to show it to him. When I said my prayers at night, I always made sure to say his name. How I always wanted to be close to him, feel his protective warmth against me as we sat in the grass or on the roof. My parents often talked to my siblings and I about how they were deeply in love with each other. But the one thing those stories didn't tell me was what it was to be in love with a boy, as a boy. I didn't think that was possible by the rules of such tales.

But just because I couldn't put a name to the feeling didn't mean it wasn't there. I followed Theodore everywhere around our town in New York. He wanted to grow up fast and be an adult, an explorer, and go wherever he wanted. I just wanted to always be able to be at his side, to see his chestnut curls bounce as he ran.

Everyday he'd make up a new game, but never told me the rules, just the roles.

"Sammy, you're my first mate on my ship. We're going to find ourselves some treasure!" or, "Let's go Lieutenant, the enemy's just over the hill. Don't worry, we'll get them together." I could never say no to him, even at a young age. His freckled smile would disarm me and fill me with energy, ready to follow him into any danger. And I always did.

We'd stay out way past when Momma wanted me home. Early on Sundays before church, he'd come by and convince me to run along with him to chat or roughhouse. One time I got my one good set of clothes dirty. Let's just say it was hard to sit through church that day. I wasn't surprised my parents were upset; I knew I only had the one set of nice clothes, but I would have traded them to have seen the glint in Theo's hazel eyes.

We weren't poor, but we just barely weren't poor. I had several siblings, some older, some younger. My parents ran a tailor shop: Momma fixed clothes, Daddy worked the front and chatted with the people who came in. Being that I was smack dab in the middle of all my siblings, I didn't get much focus, which meant I could sneak off to play with Theo. But Theo was an only child, his parents doted on him, and while they weren't rich, they just barely weren't rich. They let him run off wherever, with hardly any rules to restrain him. Theo was hard to bind with any set of rules.

With time, it became easier and easier for me to stay at his house. His parents adored me. I was quiet and polite, and in comparison to Theo's boisterous energy, they must have seen me as the calmer part of their son. My parents barely noticed; if anything they were happy when I went to stay with him. It was one less mouth to feed.

Those nights I stayed with them—unlike anything else we did—had a rhythm, a constant narrative that we couldn't deviate from. We would play outside until supper, then we read inside in his father's study (this was in his effort to be like an adult, most times I just sat and let him read to me), then we'd bathe at his mother's behest, always together. "Best not to waste the hot water," she'd say, giving no mind to how I'd started blushing and hesitating at the thought as the closer we got to our teen years.

But my favorite part was after we were clean and settled in. We would sneak out of his window to go to the nearby hill and watch the stars. The first night amazed me; the dark sky was filled with stars, like a black sheet with a bright light shining through so many holes. The Milky Way stretched across the sky like a beautiful stain. But I only paid attention to the stars the first time. Theo's face had captured my attention, the wonder and peace written so clearly, all I could do was watch him.

On chilly nights, we'd get close underneath the blanket, his warm arm pressed against mine. He'd show me the constellations, holding my fingers to point to be sure I saw where he wanted. When our hands touched, it felt natural under the light of the stars. The feeling of his warmth, the softness of his hands, and the strength in his fingers often found me in my dreams.

I'd never forget the last time it happened either. I was twelve, he was thirteen. His other friends, the richer ones, had all started talking about girls, and he didn't understand it. Why would they talk about being with a girl, when they all preferred hanging out with their guy friends and doing "guy things." Theo (a name only I could call him now—he went by Theodore by everyone else in an attempt to seem an adult) much preferred my company to any girl's.

My stomach flipped when he had said that. I still hadn't accepted how I felt for Theo. I just thought that was the way of our friendship, to feel sparks at his very touch, soothed by his endless stories. I told him I preferred his company too, over anyone else. That was the first time I saw him blush. His cheeks, thinning by the demands of puberty, reddened under his freckles. We laid there together for a moment, looking into each other's eyes, dropping the pretense of star gazing. Hazel meeting a dark brown. I glanced at our hands, my skin the color of trees, his the color of clouds, with fingers crossing.

When I looked up, he was suddenly there. His lips against mine. He lingered for a moment, his eyes squeezed shut as mine opened in surprise, then closed in joy. The moment felt cosmic, like something that was eternally dancing with the stars and loved by the moon. When he pulled away, we had left the world behind, and it was just us two floating in a galactic ocean.

Then he ran.

He took a moment as he looked at me, his whole face red and twisted with something I had never seen on it before. Confusion? Anger? Shame? He bolted back to the house, leaving me alone. He left me to crash back to earth, cold and alone beneath the unblinking eye of the moon.

I didn't know how long I stayed out there, but eventually I made my way back to his room through the window. He was in bed, pretending to be asleep, but I knew he wasn't. He snored when he was sleeping, and his breathing was calm and even now. I didn't feel right sharing a bed with him like we had always done before. My own face was burning hot and wet with tears. I shouldn't have hoped. I shouldn't have liked that simple kiss as much as I did. But all I could think about was how much I wanted another one.

But it was the only bed I could get to, so I crawled in and faced away from him, and stared at the opposite wall, both of us unspeaking and unsleeping until the sun cast the first light into the room. "You should get home," he said. "Church will start soon." Those were the last words he said to me for five years.

I spent months, years, trying to forget him, but every new friend I made reminded me. Any time something exciting happened, I wanted to tell him. I even started writing him letters that I knew I would never send. No matter how much time had passed, who I tried to court—because I did try to court a few ladies—inevitably my mind drifted back to the hazel eyes full of curiosity and mischief. The quirk of his pink lips as he smiled and the lilt and crack in his voice as he told his many stories.

In contrast to the vibrant portraiture I had in my head of Theo, I lived a gray, still life. I went to the shop and helped Momma. Daddy tried to teach me how to run the shop, but I took better to Momma's lesson on how to mend clothes. Every day blended, barely anything breaking the monotony. It wasn't a bad life by any means. My older siblings got married and moved out until I was the oldest in the house. I was given more responsibilities like taking care of the younger siblings and the shop as Momma needed a break.

I thought it was all fine, until he came back.

He strolled into the shop, as boisterous as the day he had left. "Sammy! Boy do I have a story for you." He wore a suit, dark blue against his pale, freckled skin. His hazel eyes sparkled as he smiled, a small scar just over the corner of his mouth. I missed whatever else came from his mouth as I realized there was a pretty girl hanging on his arm. Her blonde hair fell in neat curls that tumbled down her shoulders, bright blue eyes and a cute small smile. She wore a vibrant green dress, in the latest fashions that any woman in town would be jealous of.

I didn't catch what he had been talking about. I couldn't focus. I felt ill. "Who is she?"

"Oh, how rude of me," Theo said as he patted her hand with a wide smile. "This is Amelia; she's my fiancée."

All I could do was nod as he invited me to have dinner with him and Amelia that night, my heart thudding louder than his words. Eventually they left; I managed to muster enough of my sensibilities to give Amelia a proper kiss on the hand goodbye. Theo himself pulled me in with a tight embrace, as if we hadn't been separated all these years. As if we were just children and were as close as ever. "I hope we will see you tonight," he said in my ear before he let me go, took Amelia's arm and strolled out of my shop, upsetting the balance of my life forever.

Of course I went to dinner with them. I had never been able to deny Theo, and apparently that hadn't changed. It was a rich dinner, lamb with fresh vegetables, potatoes and a red wine, but I barely had the stomach for it. I sat and gave weak laughs at Amelia's jokes and Theo's stories. I couldn't get the warmth of Theo's body against mine out of my head. It was all I could think about, and how I wanted more.

So when he told me of his plan, I couldn't say no. It was crazy, following the pioneers out west, settling in a town out in the New World so they could have a new life together. He had heard of my passable skills with needle and thread at the family store and thought it would be good to start a tailor shop out there. He had become a self-proclaimed genius with finances, and so he would be able to set up and run the finances of said business. Amelia even had her own dreams out there: She wanted to be a great singer. Theo put it in her head that she could start singing in parlors and social clubs to get some exposure. Apparently, she had the voice of a songbird, but that didn't matter to me.

All I heard was I had another chance to have Theo in my life. So I took it.

In the three months since he walked into my shop, we didn't talk about what happened that night so long ago. And so, I definitely didn't have the bravery to tell him how I still thought of him every day. Of how much I had missed him. How I wished I could steal another kiss.

The wagon rattled beneath me as I gripped the leather of the reins, trying to ignore the giggles that came from the happy couple behind me.

"Theodore, stop!" Amelia's voice lilted in pleased admonishment. A squeal escaped her despite her protests and she lowered her voice to a criminally bad whisper. "He's right there."

"Oh, he doesn't mind," Theo said, voice muffled against something I didn't want to ponder on. "I bet he's gotten into a bit of trouble himself. Am I right?" I could hear the wink he gave me in his voice. I heard the ruffling of a dress and the giggle it brought up from Amelia. I felt my nails dig into my palm from around the leather reins.

"I'd much rather keep my eye on the way ahead. Don't want to get us lost." I fought to keep my voice level.

"Seems like you'll get lost with or without the distraction." Suddenly his voice was in my ear, and I nearly jumped out of my seat.

"Oh my, you're jumpier than the horses," Amelia said from just behind me. It seemed both of them decided to keep me company. Great.

"He's always been stuck in his head," Theo said as he put his arm around my shoulder. "He's probably thinking about the beautiful wide west where our future waits."

I tensed under his touch and hoped he didn't feel it. "Yeah, just thinking about the store. You really think they'll have need of a tailor out west?"

"Of course they do." He patted my chest with his other hand, letting it linger for just a second. "All matters of gentleman and ladies will be making their way out there. And they will always need to have someone to mend their travel worn clothes. There's always a need for someone who can mend clothes."

I barely focused on what he said. My heart raced against the palm of his hand, warm and heavy as it was. I looked over at him and found our eyes met, and in that moment, it felt like it was just the two of us there. Like he hadn't run away that night. That we had stayed under the stars together. That we stayed together for years and years.

"You must be really good if Theodore believes in you that much." Amelia's cheery voice pulled me out of my fantasy and back to the wagon. "I have a tear in one of my dresses, it got caught when we were packing. Do you think you could mend it when we stop for the night?"

"Of course he can!" Theo answered for me, his hand and arm leaving me as he turned to face his fiancée. The air felt brisk without his warmth. "People around town had said he was a whiz with some thread and needle."

"Oh that is just wonderful," Amelia said as she gave me a hug from behind.

I made some sound of acquiescence, and she turned back to talking to Theo. Why did I come with them? Did I not think they'd be like this the entire journey? I didn't know if I could survive this.

The only moments alone with Theo I could get were after a day's travel when we settled around the fire after dinner. And it wasn't every night, but the rare one when Amelia had a bit too much wine and went to sleep early. Theo and I were able to talk. Talk as if no time had passed. He'd make sure Amelia was asleep and as comfortable as she could be before coming back to me.

By the warmth of the dying flame, it was so easy to talk with him about what he'd been up to. I listened like we were kids again, hanging on his every word, laughing when he was funny, and drinking in the orange glow of him from across the low flames, the darkness a familiar blanket hiding us from the rest of the very heavens

But we were governed by unspoken rules that couldn't be broken in these spaces. We couldn't talk about that night when we were kids. No matter how much I thought about it. No matter how much I wondered if my hand would still fit so easily into his. No matter how badly I wanted to know what the scruffy beard he had grown felt like if I were to kiss him.

We always had to sit on opposite sides of the fire. No matter how cold the winds blew through our clothes and blankets. Or how he looked at me through the fire, the flames dancing and casting shadows on him. I couldn't walk over and hold his face in my hands, even though it was painted in shades of yearning and desire.

Any movement would disrupt the illusion that he was mine instead of Amelia's.

If I would even stand to just shake feeling back in my legs, he would startle, the gentle illusion shattered. He'd jump up and say, "Well I should probably get some rest, Sammy. Amelia doesn't sleep well without me there," and hurry back to the wagon to join his fiancée, leaving no room for a rebuttal. But even then, for just a moment before he'd jump into the back of the wagon, I saw him stop and look at me. I could feel how much he might want me. The hope that that was true kept me going. It kept me strong enough to weather our journey.

~

"Why don't you two just admit you're lost." Amelia fanned herself as she sat in the back of the wagon. Theo and I stood beside the horses, trying to determine where I had taken the wrong turn as we looked over the map we had bought in the last town. Turned out the map was worthless. We stood at a crossroads trying to decide which way to go, the summer sun blazing down on us. I was soaked through in sweat and my thin undershirt clung to my body. Theo had long given up on shirts and his bare torso had begun to turn red beneath the thin layer of dark hair that covered his chest. It took all of my concentration not to stare.

He threw his arm around my shoulders and pointed randomly at the map. "Where do you think we are, again?" His arms were firm against me, muscular and sturdy and sweat covered. His face was close to mine and as I glimpsed over, he caught my eye with the mischief ridden glint he used to have back when we were kids. It struck me speechless again. He squeezed my arm, an action of comfort, but it sent me spiraling even further.

"We left Ashland yesterday morning," Amelia said, weariness staining her voice. As she spoke, I felt Theo tense. He didn't look at me as he pulled away again to pull himself into the wagon driver's seat. "He's just a bit turned around, dearest. Back when we were kids, I was the one who took us places. He was always awful with directions."

"Didn't you also get us lost, Theodore?"

One thing I could appreciate about Amelia was that she was willing to call Theo out; something I just never had the heart to do. He held my heart, but she seemed to hold his.

"Pardon me, travelers. Would it appear that you are in need of some directional assistance?" I didn't notice how close the man had gotten until he spoke. We all jumped as he just seemed to appear behind the wagon. He was a tall, thin man, dressed head to toe in black despite the heat. His bowler hat sat on a head of shaggy black hair and he had a pair of red sunglasses on which completely obscured his eyes. It gave the appearance of a predator watching in the night.

"My apologies, I did not mean to startle you all." As he spoke, he flicked his peacoat out behind him, and gave the slightest bow. "I am Mr. Themann. My friends call me Moe."

Theo was the first one to recover himself and took steps toward Mr. Themann. "Good day, Mr. Themann. I'm sorry that you found us in such a state of undress, but you're right—we are quite lost. Sammy here gets a bit confused when it comes to reading maps."

"I am not bad at reading maps; the maps are just wrong." I walked up to join the two of them.

"Well, may I look at the map you are working with?" Mr. Themann's voice was so deep I felt more than heard it. He had a polite smile on as he held out his hand. Something about him was unsettling, but I couldn't help but listen. I handed the map over to him without another thought. It didn't take him but a few moments before he tutted at the paper. "No wonder you all got a bit turned around. This map is outdated to say the least."

"I knew that shopkeeper was a bit shifty," Amelia whispered harshly to Theo.

"Apologies, my dear," Mr. Themann said. "I do not believe your companions have yet to introduce us."

I turned to look at Theo and Amelia but was shocked to find that I met Theo's gaze. I felt my face grow warm before he turned to walk toward Amelia. He held out a hand and helped her out of the wagon.

"This lovely lady is my fiancée, Amelia." I couldn't tell if it was my imagination or not, but I think Theo hesitated on the word "fiancée." The tight smile that Amelia gave him confirmed it for me. It wasn't just in my head. My stomach twisted.

Mr. Themann took Amelia's hand and gave it a gentle kiss. "It is a pleasure to meet you, miss. Now, with you all thoroughly lost, I do have some good news. The caravan I have been travelling with should be waiting for me to catch up with them not too far from here. Would you like to join us on our journey westward? Feel free to leave whenever you would like, but traveling with a group of people is safer and much easier to keep on the right path."

"Thank you for the offer," I said before Theo could make a decision. "But I think we should be fine on our own. We don't want to impose on your group."

"What are you talking about?" Theo grabbed my wrist and pulled me back toward Amelia. "Excuse us for a moment," he called out to the stranger. "Would you mind if we just had a moment to discuss?"

"Why of course," Mr. Themann said. "But do be mindful, we should be on the road soon."

"Are you crazy?" Theo barely whispered at me as the three of us got to the other side of our wagon. He held onto my wrist, not quite firm enough to hold me in place. "We have someone who is wanting to help us, and at this point we need all the help we can get."

"Something just doesn't feel right. I just think that we should head back to town and find our way from there."

"I don't know, Samuel," Amelia piped up. "It would be better to travel with a larger group of people. It's going to get more dangerous and wild the farther west we go."

"Exactly," Theo said. "We must take every possible advantage we can. Trust me, Sammy. Even back when we were kids, I never steered us wrong."

That was factually untrue, but still I had followed him. I hadn't changed much since then. I let out a sigh, and that was all the assent Theo needed. He gave me a huge smile and slid his grasp from my wrist to my hand and squeezed as he leaned over to kiss Amelia on the cheek. Whatever reservation I held melted with that singular gesture.

"Looks like we will be joining you after all," Theo called out to the stranger-made-companion.

"Excellent," Mr. Themann said with a suggestion of a smile. "Well, let us get back on the road. I am sure the rest of the caravan is going to enjoy your company."

The caravan was made up of eight different wagons that all held what seemed to be as much as they could carry for each of the families that guided them. The people were scattered about, having already made camp for the day despite the sun still being high in the sky. On the far end, some of the men were skinning a deer that they had caught, mothers were trying to wrangle younger kids to not stray too far, and a few were just mingling.

The people all looked friendly enough; some waved, some came up to introduce themselves, all greeting Mr. Themann first. It seemed we had found a decent group of people to travel westward with. Not at all shifty like the last people we met in town.

I couldn't shake the feeling that something was off with our guide. Every time he spoke, my stomach dropped a bit. Everyone we met seemed eager to see him and reverential of him, the way one might behave around a preacher or pastor. It brought to mind tales of religious leaders taking their flock out west on God's word. Many of them were never heard from again, or worse, a single survivor made their way back to the colonies forever changed.

Any worry I felt was washed away with a sentence from Theo and a smile. "It's an adventure just like the old days."

I rolled my eyes and turned as my face flushed at the recollection of the memories. I kicked at the ember of hope in my chest that things could go back to that. Theo had to know it wouldn't, couldn't go back to that time. He was the one who had run away. He was the one who had abandoned me, and now he had a fiancée. Amelia would be the one who got to live my dream. Jealousy burned in me even though she had no clue what she had done, and it made me feel sick.

My introspection didn't last long. During the introductions around the caravan, the world shook around us. A deep rumbling sounded from within the earth as everyone began to panic. It shook hard enough to knock me off of my feet, as unsteady as I already was. I had never experienced anything like this before. Was this God's wrath? What else could cause the very ground to shake beneath us all?

"Do not worry everyone," Mr. Themann's voice rang out clear over the panic, a look of mere annoyance on his face rather than the fear the rest of us felt. He raised his arms out for a moment to calm a frightened horse, the quick motion making his black jacket look as wings for the briefest second. "This region of the West is known for having such tremors. We are safe, it will pass."

Moments later the rumbling faded away, seeming to move further out in the distance, and the ground sitting still once again. I had been shaken by such an event, and I couldn't seem to find my feet again.

"Are you alright?" I felt a tentative hand touch my forearm. It snapped me out of my thoughts and I looked up to see

Amelia standing alone in front of me. "That was quite a doozy."

I looked around for Theo. Amelia and I had yet to have a moment alone. I didn't know how to act around just her, especially when I felt shame bring heat to my cheeks as I looked up at her from the ground like a child.

"He'd gone off to help the men chop some wood before the tremors," she said, understanding my look of confusion. "Better to stockpile on wood now before we get too far west. Apparently the land gets so flat, you could see for miles."

"I heard something similar," I managed to say. Just looking at her, I felt a burn in the back of my throat as it tightened. This level of jealousy was new to me; I had always accepted my lot in life. But I wanted her to lose it all. Despite what I knew was right, I wanted her to be the one left alone out under the stars. I wanted her to know what it was like to meet the next person of Theo's affection. I wanted her to know what it was like to be utterly alone like I had.

I disgusted myself.

I turned to the wagon. "We should get what we need out of the wagon for tonight." I couldn't hide the venom in my voice.

"Oh," Amelia responded, her voice small. "You're right."

We went through the wagon in total silence. She didn't deserve such animosity, but I couldn't find a way to quell that poison in me, so I stayed quiet. Her role in his life hadn't hit me until I heard him introduce her as his fiancée over and over again. I had been delusionally hopeful that it could be different, that he'd choose me.

"You mean a lot to Theo," Amelia said quietly as she pulled some small bottles from her bag.

"What?"

"When he came up with this plan to go west, he didn't want to go without trying to get you."

"Oh." I barely made a sound. It was hard to breathe.

Amelia sat down with a sigh and shook her head with a smile. "I hadn't heard of you except for drunken stories about his childhood best friend and the adventures you two had. You know he was a good businessman, selling the ideas of inventors to larger businesses, but I think he wasted his talent. He always told the most magnificent stories. That's how I fell in love with him."

"I can imagine." I stood frozen facing the white wall of canvas. Her candor caught me off guard.

"Anyways, he would speak the world of you. 'My dearest friend,' he'd always say." She gave a quiet laugh. "Now, he has a new energy to him. He seems revitalized since we started this journey together. I just wanted to thank you. I understand you don't know me too well yet, but I hope, in time, we can become good friends as well."

It took me a moment and I nodded, quickly wiping the tears that had gathered in my eyes. "I'm sure we will, Amelia. Let's keep working. The sun is starting to dip."

When the sun touched the horizon, the caravan began lighting campfires for every family and one larger one to cook a stew over. The mothers gathered around the cooking fire and chatted as they helped chop whatever vegetables they had and cut some bread that had to be on the turning point of stale. Children laughed as they sat and listened to stories from their fathers. Those without the responsibilities of children began drinking and sharing their own stories with each other.

Naturally this meant that Theo had brought Amelia and I to meet some of the other younger adults to share a drink. There were five others around the fire with us as we passed around several bottles of whisky and wine that warmed our bodies and loosened our tongues. It seemed to be another unspoken rule found around this fire that if the bottle was passed to you, you had to at least sip from it. It would be considered rude to deny the gifts of these people who welcomed us in. They asked what brought us out this way, and of course Theo spun them a story. Told them of his dreams of having his girl and best friend starting a life all together. A story of dreams and riches to be.

I rolled my eyes. I'm sure everyone would abandon and ignore their best friend for five years. I felt the warmth in my chest turn to a fire and everything tilted for a moment. Theo kept talking but I couldn't make sense of them as my head swam. I had maybe a bit too much of the drink, and I needed to get away for a moment.

I pushed myself to my feet and felt the whole world tilt again as I took a stumbling step away from the fire. I caught my balance and made my way beyond the light of the fire and past the wagons. I stumbled into the darkness and sat myself at the top of a nearby hill. The sounds of the caravan muted and I laid back in the grass. I closed my eyes to try to still the spinning that had taken hold of my head. I focused on the grass beneath me, let my fingers run through it as it tickled my palms.

The spinning finally stopped and I opened my eyes to find myself greeted by the wide night sky. The stars danced in the swirling blackness to a cosmic melody I couldn't hear and it made me feel like a child again. All those nights in the open air, just chill enough to get goosebumps, and my eyes to water. The only thing missing was—

"There you are," Theo called out and I felt warmth wash over me. It was as if he knew I was thinking of him.

I turned to look at him, silhouetted against the darkness, and for a moment I thought he was a kid, untamable curls with an adventurous look in his eyes. I blinked and he was the adult I still cared for. His curls were now cut short, his frame now tall and firm. But his eyes remained the same, adventurous and wild. I could tell even in the dim moonlight.

He draped the blanket he brought over me and sat just out of reach. I wrapped the blanket around myself and sat up. “Where’s Amelia?”

“I brought her to the wagon to get some rest. The wine had gotten to her head and she needed some rest.” Theo smiled. “She’s fast asleep now. Even doing her little snore.”

I gave him a dry chuckle. She never would admit that she snored, but there were many nights where Theo and I heard her make sounds like a small puppy. “If only there was a way we could get her to hear herself. It’s just... it’s kind of...”

“Cute.” Theo looked up at the stars. I felt the ember burn in the pit of my stomach.

I laid back down, bringing the blanket over me as the grass tickled the back of my neck. I saw him copy me in my peripheral, still out of reach.

We laid there together in silence. I was unfamiliar with the rules of this situation and I didn’t really care. The wine, whisky and stars seemed to have washed away so much of the worry I always held onto. I felt as if the only thing holding me down to the earth was the blanket. It smelled of wood smoke.

“This reminds me of back then.” Theo finally broke the silence.

“Back then?” I gathered my thoughts to focus on his words. It was much more difficult than I thought.

“Back when we were kids.” There was something in his voice I couldn’t place. It made me want to grab his hand. I gripped the grass instead.

“Those used to be my favorite nights. When we would spend nights together. Everyone always expected something from me. I... well, I had to play into it.”

I was afraid to say anything, scared it would shock him out

of whatever sentimentality he was feeling. I turned to face him and nodded. He kept his gaze to the sky, as he ran a hand up his arm. "You never expected anything from me. You always just let me take us on adventures and be loud and annoying and quiet and sad. I don't think anyone has ever known me as well as you did."

He turned to look at me and I could see his eyes were moist. He gave me a smile, one I hadn't seen before. It was fragile, just on the verge of shattering. The ember inside me went out. I lifted the blanket and extended my arm.

"You're cold. Come under the blanket with me."

There was a moment of stillness.

Then he got up, took a few steps, and settled underneath the blanket next to me. Our knees touched and I felt a warmth wash over me. Our hands brushed against each other in the hidden space we had created. Hidden from wandering eyes and stars. His face was inches away from me. As he breathed, I smelled whisky and wine. I saw the wetness in his eyes mixed with a pain I hadn't previously seen.

"I missed you." Those three words grabbed my heart. His finger began to trace circles against the back of my palm. It caused so many emotions to swell inside me that finally let me ask a question that I had wondered for years.

"Then why did you leave?"

"I was scared."

"Of me?"

"No...'

"Then of what?" I felt the heat rise to my chest. It burned hot, but it didn't hurt.

"I didn't know how I was supposed to feel. We are supposed to have girlfriends and wives. You were supposed to just be a friend, but..."

"But you wanted more?"

He nodded.

"I do too." I slid our fingers together, intertwined. He didn't pull away. He always led our adventures. He was the one who always ran into the unknown. The last time, he kissed me. It was time I took the lead.

I leaned in and kissed him and something in my chest exploded. It warmed me as if my skin had never met sunshine, as if I had never even known the warmth a single piece of coal could produce. It burned through me and left only one thought left in my body. *I need him.*

I took a breath and looked him in the eyes as I pulled back. The same fire burned in him. His eyes hungered for more. More of me. I never thought I would see such a look from him.

He kissed me and we went up in flames. My hands traveled over parts of him I only kept in my dreams. I felt the way his stomach tightened under my touch. Over through the hairs of his chest and up to his neck before he gave way and took his shirt off. I followed. No one had ever seen me in such a state and a part of my mind dulled with anxiety. *What if he doesn't like what he sees? Am I good enough for him?*

He kissed down my neck and it shut all other thoughts away. I could only focus on the feeling of his body against mine. His skin, his lips, his hair. I didn't realize when we had both stripped our pants off, but we were as close as we could be, every inch of him against me. I kissed him like he was air, and I couldn't breathe.

I felt parts of him that only a lover could know. Our bodies shivered in a way that had nothing to do with the cool, night air. In knowing we became one: we breathed as one, felt as one, moved as one. The heat between us continued to climb, burning hot and bright like the sun.

Then, suddenly, I was bare beneath the night sky. Every

part of me exposed to the stars as Theo breathed heavily several steps away.

"Theo?" I was disoriented. I still felt as we and not as me. I tried to sort out what had happened. Theo's pale skin glistened slightly in the moonlight and I could see his wide eyes filled with panic.

"No. No, I can't do this."

I got to my knees and reached for his hand. "What're you talking about?" As soon as my hand touched his, he pulled away from me.

"This was a mistake. I... I need to go see Amelia."

My delusion shattered. This wasn't meant to be. There would always be Amelia. And we both had betrayed her tonight. Whatever flame I had left me, and all I had was the bitter cold grasp of night.

"Of course," I said.

He slid on his underclothes, grabbed the rest, and ran back to our wagon. To his Amelia.

I laid back down in the grass naked. I looked up at the stars as they looked at me. I wept.

I don't know when I fell asleep, but I eventually awoke at the top of the hill alone. My clothes were strewn to the side where I had left them and I felt a hollow. It had happened. Again. As it would likely always be. He would never choose me.

I got dressed and watched the horizon. The sun rose behind a thick layer of gray clouds that grew ever dark. A storm was coming. I took a breath. Took another. Then made my way back to the caravan.

Waiting for me at the outskirts was Mr. Themann. He leaned against one of the wagons and smoked from a pipe; dark clouds floated away from him like they had a mind of their own.

"Had a long night?" Mr. Themann asked, not unkindly.

"Yes. I did. I'd like to get back to my wagon."

"Go right ahead, Mr. Hughes. Best get ready for the day. Quite the storm is brewing."

I nodded and walked past him to our wagon. Most of the caravan was beginning to stir, people packing up their belongings. Even Amelia was awake and stirring porridge over a small fire. I didn't know how to approach her. Did Theo tell her what had happened? Would she be furious with me? I had betrayed the trust she had just given to me. What kind of person did that make me?

"Good morning, Sammy. Are you hungry?" Her chipper tone told me everything. She didn't know.

"No, thank you. My stomach is upset. Too much drink last night." Only half a lie. Guilt twisted what was left of my hollow insides as much as any alcohol could.

"Well you should still get something on your stomach. It'll help you settle. Go in the wagon and get yourself a piece of bread. I know Theodore told us to ration, but this can stay our little secret." She gave me a wink and my stomach twisted even farther.

"Is he still asleep?" I could barely speak.

"Yeah, he always sleeps in after a heavy night of drinking." She continued to stir her small pot. "I'm glad he got me to bed. He's just a sweetheart, isn't he?"

I said nothing as I made my way to the back of the wagon. Maybe this poisoned feeling inside of me would fade away with time. I could hope. Once we got to a town and settled in, once Theo and Amelia had a few children and were happy. Maybe then the feeling would disappear.

I didn't know then that the feeling would change to something entirely new.

When I climbed into the wagon, I saw Theo sprawled out toward the front, still in his underclothes and gently snoring.

In that moment I felt the hollow space inside me fill with an unfamiliar poison. I had disliked people, even hated some, but this feeling had never been directed toward Theo. No matter what he had done before, I always forgave him. But this time I felt something slither inside of me that called to violence as I watched him quietly snore.

He had abandoned me again. He let me think he cared and he left me alone under the stars once again. What's worse is that I'd let myself believe that it could have been more. That I was finally getting what I wanted with a man promised to someone else. And I'd let myself believe that. I had fallen into the fantasy he didn't know he had created.

I walked over to him, watching him sleep as if there wasn't a worry in the world. I kicked him. Not hard enough to hurt, but hard enough to make sure he felt it.

"Huh, what's going on?" Theo jumped up from his sleep.

"Amelia made you breakfast. Go eat."

When he realized I was there, he tensed. He looked anywhere but me as he stood up and pulled on his shirt. Was he really just going to not say anything about what happened?

"Right. Thank you." He began to move past me, clearly ready to be far away from me.

"Is that all you have to say?"

"Is there anything I'm supposed to say, Samuel?"

I didn't respond. I couldn't remember the last time he called me by anything other than Sammy. Even in my anger, the pain stunned me.

"What happened last night," Theo said, his voice low as he looked over his shoulder. "Well, it didn't happen. It couldn't have happened. And it won't happen again. I'm engaged to Amelia. That's that."

I stared at him, wanting him to look me in the eye when he shattered my heart again, but he couldn't even do that. I wanted to explode. I wanted to pour out every ounce of venom within me and make him take it all. But before I could even say anything, I heard one of the other men yell out, "Pack up everyone. Let's head out before this storm hits."

The rest of the caravan packed up faster than I would have thought possible. They were well practiced in a quick evacuation. Even the families with a hodgepodge of children were able to get them together and ready to go within the half hour. Theo, on the other hand, was moving as if his feet were glued to the dirt. He complained about his head throbbing and how he was nauseated, but quite frankly I was glad. I shouldn't have been the only one who was hurting after last night. I had no sympathy for him, no matter how my heart hurt.

In the end we were able to pack everything away and get our horses ready in time for us to trail the caravan from behind, just as the storm reached us. The sky was a roiling blanket of dark gray, with winds whipping across the plains like angry spirits determined to scour the earth of anything but the dead dirt beneath us.

"The weather's getting real nasty out there," I heard Theo say from inside the wagon.

I chose not to respond.

"Well, you know this area is prone to such terrible windstorms," Amelia said. "It was only a matter of time before one came across our path."

A gust of wind battered against the canvas causing it to snap harshly and nearly fly off the wagon itself. The noise scared the horses into a frenzy, and it took everything I had to hold the reins to keep them on the path.

"What's going on?" Theo said as he appeared by my side. "Do you need any help with them?"

"No, I got it," I snapped. It was hard enough to get the horses to follow the rest of the caravan, I didn't need Theo getting in the way. “Why don’t you go back to your wife, Theodore.“

I saw him recoil at my use of his full name. Good. He wanted to pretend nothing happened; I could pretend like nothing happened.

He hesitated for a moment. It was clear there was something else that he wanted to say. As he went to speak, he stopped and squinted at something in the distance. “What is that?” I spared a glimpse to where he was looking as I continued to wrangle the horses, and my jaw dropped. Amongst the roiling blanket of gray, a twisting column had begun to reach down for the ground just over the hill to the right of the caravan

“What is—”

“Tornado!” A voice from the caravan screamed and everything was chaos.

People abandoned their wagons. Some families whipped their horses to try to run away. I was frozen in place. I had seen some bad weather—blizzards and rainstorms often flew over my old home—but I had never seen anything like this. It was the hand of God reaching down to us. And when the clouds touched the ground, there was a ripping sound louder than anything I’d ever heard. Trees and plants alike were yanked from the ground and tossed about like they weighed no more than a cloud.

I heard voices screaming around me, but I couldn’t understand what they were saying. Then, Theo was there again, pulling at me. “We have to go. Please, Sammie, let’s go!” I could barely hear him over the approaching tornado as it tore across the countryside.

I looked past him and saw Amelia watching us halfway up the hill behind him, fear written across her face mingled with what I thought to be anger. She was waiting for Theo and Theo wouldn't leave without me.

I jumped from the wagon and Theo grabbed my hand and started running. Even amidst the chaos, his touch burned to me and I snatched my hand away before running ahead of him to Amelia. "Keep running, Amelia!" She wasted no time listening. She hiked up her skirts and ran faster than I had seen her run before.

The tornado was rushing toward us, throwing all sorts of debris all around. A large branch from a broken tree speared into the ground, missing me by a few feet as I reached the top of the hill. It made me trip over myself, and I started sliding down back the other end. There had to be somewhere we could take cover. We couldn't outrun this forever.

I hit the bottom of the hill and Amelia immediately helped me to my feet. I ran after her, constantly looking up to be sure there would be no further falling debris coming at us. I paused at the dark maw of a cave that loomed before us. It was a solid wall of darkness and while I had never been scared of the dark, a primal part of me rejected going into such a space. Amelia ran into it, swallowed by the shadows, her nerves stronger than my own.

There had to be another option. Going into the bowels of the earth to escape the wrath of the sky felt like jumping out of the frying pan and into the fire.We hadn't seen any caves this whole journey in the hilly plains, why was there one here right when we needed one?

I didn't have any time to consider as I felt something collide with my back, launching me bodily into the darkness. My face hit the ground, and I saw stars. I didn't know which way was up. Then someone landed on top of me, a prompt reminder of which way down was. But even that was muted by the thunderous crash that shook the ground around us. The only light was snuffed out by the rubble and dirt falling around us.

"Are you alright?" Theo said inches from my ear. Of course it was him who knocked me down. And now he was laying on top of me, pinning me to the ground. If he wanted this, he should have done it last night.

"Get off me," I grunted. I shoved my elbow into him as I got up. He moved off me, and I heard him shuffle to his feet. I looked around in the darkness; a limited light changed the surrounding blackness to a barely discernible gray. Amelia had collapsed against the wall a few feet ahead of me. I could hear her breathing in small, ragged bursts. Theo crawled over to her, following the sound of her breath with outstretched hands. She made a sound of surprise and Theo made small noises to soothe her. She grasped onto him, tightly folding into him, the emotions overtaking her now that she felt safe.

I turned away from the scene, the jealousy slowly eating away inside of me. I made my way to the entrance and felt what blocked most of the opening. It was rough and I could hear the rustle of leaves and twigs snapping in the rapid winds outside. The tornado must have thrown a tree and Theo pushed me out of the way just in time to not be crushed. He had saved my life. A part of me felt hope rise in me, fighting against the bitterness I was now desperate to keep. I didn't want to forgive him. Not yet, and maybe not ever.

I pushed against the fallen tree, and it sat as if it was still rooted deep into the ground. "There's no way we are going to get out the way we came in," I said. "It looks like the cave goes deeper; maybe there's another way out."

"Shouldn't we stay put and wait for the tornado to pass?" Theo asked.

"And then what? We still won't be able to move the tree."

"Well maybe the rest of the caravan will find us. It's better to just stand and wait—"

"For fuck's sake, Theo," I snapped. "We are trapped in here. The caravan was thrown into chaos by a damned tornado. They aren't going to be looking for us anytime soon. Be brave for once in your life and do something for someone else. Do you want us to wait here? Okay, for how long? Until we starve or die of thirst? Is that what you promised Amelia in your proposal?"

There was no response. In the dim light I saw him sit tense, head bowed. He was embarrassed. Good.

"He's right, darling." I didn't expect Amelia to agree with me. "We might as well keep moving on. It'll be a little adventure. Just like the stories you'd tell." There was something tight in her voice. It wasn't exactly fear. She was battling something else right now, she didn't even try to defend Theo from my reprimands.

"Fine." Theo sounded hurt, defeated. "How are we going to see?"

Good point. We had no supplies to start a fire.

"Does it matter?" Amelia said, standing to her feet. Her fit of fear was thrown to the side with a plan in sight. "We have to move. We will just move carefully in the dark."

A bit of admiration swelled in my chest for Amelia.

Theo stood up without a word. His demeanor had shifted, now unsure and scared. Something I hadn't seen from him except by the light of the stars.

I patted his shoulder as I walked past him. "Let's go, captain," I said, words echoing from childhood. "Maybe there's treasure ahead."

There was no treasure.

Only an endless darkness. Our eyes adjusted to the lack of light enough to see the outlines of each other and the walls.

But after half an hour of walking, even the faintest remnants of light had faded. It was a true darkness to which our eyes could never acclimate. We traced the rough rock and earth walls and tried to listen for anything that might give us any hint of where we were headed.

After what might have been the third hour, my eyes played tricks on me. There were moments where I thought I saw movement, something scurrying ahead of me. It did not help that the only sounds we heard were our own footsteps, and the occasionally scurry of some small underground creature.

Then, a deep groaning and grinding sound vibrated through the tunnel. At first it was quiet and short. Then again, louder as it caused the tunnel to shake.

There was a sudden burst of air and an explosion of rocks that knocked me back into Amelia. Something tore through the earth and rock as if it were paper. The sound of its grinding was deafening. For a moment, the cave was illuminated by sickly jade light that shone from the creature. I was barely able to glimpse whatever it was that nearly decimated me; it was a solid wall of undulating flesh beneath the glow. For the second time that day, I was horrified into silence.

And just as quick as it appeared, it was gone. It left a glowing ooze in the new tunnel it had bored perpendicular to the path we were taking. I turned and looked Amelia in the eyes and it snapped her out of her paralyzed fear, giving way for her next course of action: to scream.

She let out a hair-raising screech that echoed through the tunnels before Theo clapped a hand over her mouth. I listened for a moment; the grinding groan had disappeared and didn't seem to be coming back.

"What the hell was that?" Theo whispered.

I couldn't answer. I'd never seen a creature that big in my life. I turned to look back at whatever slime it left, the glow already dimming. I scooped a small bit onto my finger. It was hot to the touch, but was cooling quickly. .

"We have to keep going," I said.

"What the hell do you mean? With that...that thing down here?" Theo said, his voice barely staying a whisper.

"We either move forward and maybe find a way out, or we stay here and wait for it to come back. And next time, it probably won't miss."

As the ooze began to lose its glow, Theo and I stared at each other. There was defiance bred from fear in his eyes. He didn't want to follow me because he never had to before. He didn't think I could get us to safety.

Amelia took a breath to calm herself before fruitlessly dusting off her already ruined dress. She walked over to me and grabbed my arm. "I'll follow you." I watched Theo's face turn from defiant to defeated in the last of the light.

We marched on in total silence. The only way we knew where we were was by holding onto each other with one hand and to the wall with the other. Amelia followed behind me, her grip tight on my shirt, and behind her, Theo.

Eventually Amelia spoke up, her voice earth-shatteringly loud after the long silence. "I need to rest for a bit. Maybe we can call it a day and get some sleep here?"

Theo gave a non-committal grunt which was followed by rocks scattering. I felt the tug of Amelia as she lowered herself to the ground. I followed her down cautiously. The soil beneath us was softer than I had thought; it called for me to just lay down and sleep. But I knew Amelia needed some rest more than me. She asked for it after all.

"If you two want to get some rest, I can stay up just to keep an ear out for anything."

"Do you think that thing will come back?" Amelia asked, exhausted.

"It'll come back, it's just a matter of when." Theo's voice was devoid of any of his signature spark. He had already given up.

"Well, it might," I said, not wanting to lie. "I'm hoping I'll be able to hear it before it does. Get some warning so it doesn't catch us by surprise again."

"We'll see."

It wasn't long before I heard Theo's breathing turn into light, rhythmic snores. My mind wandered to a future out of these caves. What was left for me now that the unrealistic hope I had built up was now gone? Theo and Amelia would settle into their routine, Amelia trying to sing at different saloons to build a reputation. Theo would work to set up the business where I would work as the tailor. Theo and Amelia would have children, growing happily together. Would I find someone else? Would it be another secret romance, only meant to bloom beneath the watchful eye of the moon? Could I have anything more?

"Um... Samuel, are you still awake?" Amelia spoke in a gentle whisper.

"Yes. Why are you? Get some rest." I matched her whisper, not wanting to wake Theo from his sleep. But even the whispers seemed to go too far in this space.

"I know, but I just couldn't sleep." There was something unsaid in the air.

"Don't listen to Theo. We'll get out of here."

"Oh what? No, no that's not what's on my mind." She shifted closer to me, our arms now pressed against each other, confirmation we were both there in total nothingness. A moment of silence lapsed between us, broken only by Theo's heavy breathing.

"I know about Theodore," she finally said. I hoped she couldn't hear how hard my heart was beating. Did she know about me and Theo last night? Did Theo tell her?

"Theodore has always been kind and sweet to me, but I could tell there was something he hid about himself. I'm not blind. After a bit of drinking, he'd come back disheveled, sometimes smelling of a cologne I know he didn't own and, well, sometimes not even in his own clothes."

I stayed silent. I didn't want to lie to her, but what could I say? How could I make this better?

"Samuel. I don't care about that." She laid her hand on my forearm and squeezed. The heat from her palm seeped into me. "I love Theodore. Oh I love him with all my heart. If he happens to care for men as well as women, well I don't give a damn. All I care about is that he loves me. I told him as much, after I caught him the second time. We wanted to come out West as a new start. He promised me he would be mine and only mine." There was a tightness in her voice. I couldn't see her, but I knew she was crying. The guilt that built in my throat caused tears to build in the corner of my own eyes.

"He insisted you come, though. He said he needed his oldest friend with him. He said it was for the business he wanted to start with you. But I knew there was more. Something in the way he said it. How he *needed* you."

"I don't know why—"

"Please don't," Amelia said with a sigh. "Don't lie to me now. Don't lie to me like Theodore has. You're kind, I've learned that much about you. I can see why he... why he loves you too."

My heart stopped. He *loved* me? He didn't. He couldn't. He couldn't abandon someone he loved. Not twice.

"I'm going to ask you. I'm begging you... just tell me the truth. Samuel, please. Did Theodore... did he sleep with you as well?"

I flinched at it being voiced aloud. She moved her hand

from me and went rigid before she scooted over. She took a deep, shaking breath. "That told me everything. Thank you." There was a long moment of silence. "I want to be angry with you. Part of me is. But deep down, I know you aren't the person to blame. We both loved someone who decided to never give us all of himself."

I wanted to reach out to her. I wanted to do something to show her how sorry I was. I didn't want to hurt her and hadn't meant to ruin her life. But on some level I knew what I was doing. I knew what would happen. "I'm sorry, Amelia."

"So am I."

We sat in silence for a while. I realized Theo had stopped snoring. He didn't say anything and made no move to show that he had heard, but I knew. No matter what happened, we would not be leaving these tunnels as the same people we were when we came in.

I didn't know when I fell asleep, but I awoke to Theo shaking Amelia and me. "Hurry, get up. It's coming!" The panic in his voice washed away any tiredness I felt and I heard that horrid rock grinding, loud and close.

I went to pull Amelia to her feet, but I felt her dress brush past me as she whispered, "Run."

All three of us ran blindly down the tunnel. The ground shook and we stumbled, barely keeping on our feet. The flash of jade illuminated our path as the creature burst through the wall of the tunnel, mere feet behind us. Its glowing ooze gave us just enough light to see the intersection of tunnels ahead of us.

"Which way do we go?" Amelia asked, gasping for air.

Theo didn't even answer, he kept running down the right tunnel. Without a choice, I pulled Amelia along with me to follow him. I couldn't catch my breath as we ran. All I had to go off of was the sound of Theo's feet and the horrid grinding behind us. I heard Amelia behind me, barely keeping up, barely staying on her feet.

The beast erupted through the wall again, even closer than before. Its slime splashed onto my face, burning and bright. The smell of glowing byproducts of the creature was horrendous. It was rot and mildew and manure. Then I was nearly knocked off my feet as Amelia rushed into me, sending us both reeling in my attempt to keep us from touching the creature.

Amelia scrambled at my clothes to pull me closer to her, away from the monster. Suddenly the creature was gone and we saw Theo. His chest heaved for want of air and his eyes were wild. He took a step toward us, tentative as he tried to catch his breath. Then suddenly he was with us, embracing us in a hug. Amelia moved to hug him back, and I heard the beginnings of sobs in his throat.

"I thought it had gotten you," he cried in my ear. I didn't know who that was meant for.

I didn't respond. Amelia said nothing and held on to us with a grip like iron. Her body shook as she tried to take deep breaths. I wanted to cry. I wanted to sob and weep and fall apart, but the fear and anger I had been feeling hallowed me out. There was little left I could do now but observe and survive.

I pulled myself away from the two of them, pressing my back against the wall of the cave as I wiped the creature's slime off my face. Amelia looked at me with resignation in her eyes before turning back to Theo. She held his face before she checked over him to make sure he was alright. But Theo only stared at me. He watched me as if he were scared I would disappear if he blinked as the light faded.

I wanted to reach out to him again but knew I couldn't. I wouldn't do that to Amelia again. Before I could even move to make any decision, I felt the floor beneath me vibrate. It was small at first. I lowered myself to the ground, pressing my ear against to listen. For a moment I heard nothing. The vibrations on the ground stopped.

"Samuel, what are you doing?" Amelia asked.

"Shhh." I focused on listening. Something wasn't right. I felt the vibrations again, this time stronger. Then I heard it. That grinding sound, louder, faster than before coming from below.

"It's coming from below!" I scrambled to reach them. I had to try and push them out of the way. Now they could hear it as it sang through the earth around us. In the last of the light from the ooze, I watched as Theo and Amelia tried to get to their feet. The earth beneath them started to buckle from the creature's movement. Theo shoved Amelia at me. She landed at my feet with a thud and Theo took two steps. Then the creature erupted from the ground.

Theo's body was lifted until he hit the top of the ceiling with a sickening ripping. When he hit the ground again, both legs were missing from the upper thigh. The roar of the grinding drowned out any scream Theo made as he laid on the ground in misery. I watched, willing my body to move to him, but couldn't get it to move any closer to the beast as it tunneled.

Then, just as suddenly as it had appeared, it was gone. It must have broken through above ground as moonlight poured into the cave. And with the light came his screams. Theo screamed in agony as he writhed on the ground. His own blood poured out of him like wine from a broken pitcher.

My own legs were now freed from the grip of terror. I ran to Theo, collapsed next to him and pulled him into my lap as he screamed and wept. I shushed and tried to calm him as I stroked his hair, unsure of what to do. I turned to see Amelia staring at the two of us, heartbreak and horror written in equal measure on her face.

"What do I do?" I called to her; salty tears slipped into my mouth. When had I started crying?

She shook her head, voice catching in her throat. "I-I don't know. I can't... No." She stumbled backward. One step, two, before wandering off into the darkness, leaving Theo and I alone. His blood painted the ground crimson.

He had stopped screaming, his eyes unfocused as he held onto me tightly. "Sammie. Sammie, I'm sorry."

"No stop," I said, stroking his hair down. He was slick with sweat and he was cold. "It's ok. It's ok."

"No, it's not." He swallowed hard. "I brought you out here, knowing you would say yes. I hoped. Hoped that I can see you again. That I could have you in my life again."

"It's fine," I lied. "It was time I got out of my parent's house anyway." I tried to give a laugh, but it came out a choked whimper.

Theo lifted his hand and pressed it against my face. I could feel the sticky warmth of his blood. "I wish... I wish I could have done it differently." Theo's focus was fading away. His breathing was getting shallower.

"Do what differently?"

"Our nights under the stars," he said. A tear spilled from his eye. "I wish I could have a hundred more of them with you."

"Theo." All I could do was choke out his name, the anger I had felt long given way to sorrow and heartbreak again. Even as he was dying, he could still hurt me.

"I need you to know," his voice was a whisper now. "I've loved you. Ever since we were kids."

I wanted to argue with him. He couldn't have loved me. He left me *twice*, he ignored me for years. He got engaged to

Amelia. He never had the heart to tell me how he felt before and now he wanted to burden me with this as he was about to leave me again.

"I know," I whispered. Another lie. They came easier now than truths.

"I'm scared. I don't want to die." More tears slipped down his face, carving tracks through the dried dirt. I wipe them away with my thumb gently as I kissed his forehead, not knowing what else to do.

We sat there in silence for a moment. I listened as his breathing got fainter and fainter.

"Sammie..."

"Yes?"

"Can you kiss me? We can have... a proper goodbye?"

I barely held back the whimper of a cry, but I nodded. I leaned over him and pressed my lips against his. They were cold and rough, and tasted like dirt. "Goodbye, Theo."

He never responded.

I held him long after his last breath had left. Long after his heart stopped beating and his blood had soaked into my pants.

Eventually, I heard footsteps. Amelia walked into the light, her dirt ridden face streaked with tears and her eyes red and puffy. Her arms were wrapped around herself.

"Is he..." She let the question trail off, not wanting to say the truth aloud.

"Yes," I responded. I laid him down on the ground gently. Not wanting to wake him from his eternal slumber.

We were quiet for a moment.

She shuffled a step closer. "What were his last words?"

"He said, 'Tell Amelia that I loved her.'" The lie rolled off my tongue quickly and without much thought and she knew it. A tear slipped down her face as she shook her head. She took a deep, heart-wrenching breath.

"Thank you." She walked over and knelt next to me. She looked over Theo's body and I could see layers of hurt that she was buried under. So much so that the grief didn't even have time to breathe. I reached out to take her hand, and she didn't move it away. I gave it a squeeze and she squeezed it back.

In the light that poured through from above, a shadow flickered. I looked up and watched as a small black moth flitted its way through the light before landing on Theo's chest. I watched it with a detached curiosity. It seemed familiar and yet so alien to me.

I reached out to it, but it flew back through the hole above us just as I heard a voice call out from overhead. I couldn't believe my ears at first, so I looked to Amelia, who had clearly heard it too. She pushed herself to her feet and started yelling for help. I joined in, screaming at the top of my lungs. We were so close to being free.

A rope dropped down followed by a man from the caravan. I couldn't remember his name, but it didn't matter. I told him we had to leave. There was something in these caves. It killed Theo. I don't know if he believed me or not, but seeing Theo's body, he certainly rushed us all up the rope. The brightness of the sun blinded and I felt the breeze on my face. The vastness of the blue sky dotted with clouds was one of the most beautiful things I had ever seen.

I took a breath of clean fresh air. Then another. Then I felt the damn in me break as a sob tore itself out of my throat. I was safe. Amelia was safe. Theo was gone.

SOMETHING SOMETHING, WESTERN

EERIE MAEYFLOWER

Their image was warped by the heat, but Reid could make out two figures riding over. He'd been fixing a downed fence that a startled longhorn had rolled into, but now he was fixing for trouble. Tossing his tools down into the boggy dirt, he readjusted his hat and placed both of his ranch-hardened hands on his hips.

The two cowboys stopped their horses a mere five feet from him—a statement's distance. He squinted up. Reid had never seen the two before; he'd been new to town as of just last year. There were loads of curious folk, unfortunate faces, and so many big personalities that one tends to forget a few along the way. These two, however, were a pair he was sure he would have remembered.

The one on the left wore a shit-eating grin. He looked like a real charmer, with his embroidered pinched front and fancy blouse. Reid assumed the strong scent of flowery nonsense was coming from him.

The one on the right was staring Reid down with such hellish intensity that Reid tried to recall if he'd drowned anyone's dog as of late. The cowboy wore a dark duster and pushed the front flap off to one side, showcasing the awfully impressive Remmington in its holster.

Never one to be intimidated, Reid stood tall and proud. Decades of tussling with cattle had shaped Reid into a rather burly man, with a five o'clock shadow that even the sun itself couldn't penetrate. "Can I help you fellas?"

"You know Laureline Harper?" Bit the sharp eyed one, voice dripping with venom.

The smarmy one cut himself into the conversation, "Now, Sam, let's not get too ahead of ourselves." Offering Reid a true, Southern salesman's smile. "Sir, my name is Jed, and this here is my good friend Sam."

Reid nodded to the both of them. "There a problem with your good friend's eyes?"

Jed leaned into his saddle, peering over at his partner before laughing with his whole being. "I apologize, mister," wiping tears from his eyes, "Don't mind Sam. You see, we just came back into town after being away for some time. We stopped by Clancy's." Flicking his hand out to Sam, "We always stop by Clancy's. Anyway, that old waterin' hole is a great place to catch up on the town's happenin's, and we heard the strangest rumor, ain't that right, Sam?" Sharply kissing his teeth.

"Do you know Laureline Harper?" Sam asserted.

Again, Jed interrupted, "Now, Sam, I said hold on!" With a heavy sigh, he addressed Reid once more. "We heard some upsettin' news; got Sam all riled up. You see, Laureline Harper is a dear friend of ours. And now, I ain't some loose-lipped vagrant," palm to his chest, "but someone confided in us that she was havin' a hard time with a certain newcomer cattle rancher on the southeast side of town. There ain't really too many cattle ranchers on this end of the river, but we still thought we'd just do the civilized thing of asking first." Punctuating his statement with another laced smile.

At this point, Reid had pieced together that they didn't want him talking to Ms. Laura Whoever. Point taken. "Alright, gentlemen," lifting his hands dismissively, "I think I know who you're talking about. She's a very feathered-out piece of calico and I'm not trying to disrespect any man. I'd just arrived in Millbrooke not but a year ago and she was always alone. A lady like that really catches your eye; would make any fella want to know her better."

Faster than Jed could even think to interject, Sam whipped out that impressive revolver and fired at both of Reid's kneecaps. The shattering of bone and flesh wet the dusty earth with a burst of red and seeding it with bits of crunchy white.

"OH GOD!" Reid cursed as he,unceremoniously, collapsed to the ground, clutching at both limbs.

Unfazed by the pained cries, Sam holstered her gun, "Well you'd best not know her anymore."

"Just these, please," Setting her items down on the countertop.

The shopkeeper looked each one over, making a neat note of it on his inventory sheet. "Are you sure this is going to be enough?" Tallying her total on his fancy register machine.

She rummaged around in her pocketbook, looking for some change. "I'm not sure what you mean, Joe." Smiling through her confusion. "I couldn't eat more than that without something spoiling on me."

The shopkeeper leisurely corrected her, "Mr. Daybrit works just fine, Ms. Harper." Readjusting his glasses. "You normally buy more than this whenever Mr. Clay is in town. I was merely making sure I wasn't losing a sale. If you're buying cornmeal from that new Fuller Company, I am obligated by decency to inform you that their supplier mixes it with ground up oats."

All she heard was "Clay" before her mind started racing. "You saw Sam?"

Mr. Daybrit nodded, "I take it you haven't? That's very odd. He came in some time ago. He was with his friend, Mr. Pierce, of course. They bought some wine, which I thought was awfully redundant because then they went over to Clancy's and... Uh, Ms. Harper?"

Stealing the pencil out of his hand, Laureline pulled a piece of paper from her purse and scribbled instructions. "Have these items delivered." Taking out a dollar and some random change, she placed the money and the chicken scratch list down in front of him. "Thanks, Joe." She then left the store in a hurry.

He tried calling after her, "It's Mr. Dayb—! Oh, nevermind."

The sun had long since passed its highest point by the time Laureline made it home. What would have normally been a peaceful stroll through the mystic enchantments of the Louisiana backwood had instead consisted of Laureline pulling up on the layered skirt of her day dress just to keep the dang thing from tripping her up while running.

Instead of smelling like wildflowers and honeycomb, the distinct coppery perfume of the bayou had mixed with her sweat. Mud was caked onto her nice walking boots and her hair, too fine to keep a complicated style on a good day, was dangling in a low and tired bun. Maybe, if this were some years ago when she'd first met Sam, Laureline would have felt more self-conscious about her presentation.

The first time they'd met, Sam could hardly string two words together without going red. That was to be expected, though. Laureline had worn her most successful, green evening dress. It cinched the waist and made everything look like it just might spill over whenever she, strategically, bent down. While originally purchased to expand her circle of well-off *gentlemen*, Laureline had attracted someone a little bit different.

Laureline had quickly realized that it never mattered what she was wearing, how she smelled, or even what came out of her mouth. Sam would be awestruck regardless.

As she walked up the weathered porch steps, Laureline smiled ear to ear. Sam was fast asleep in a rocking chair—feet roosted up on the railing that needed repairing. There was a hat on Sam face to block out the dipping sun and her arms were folded across herself.

Creeping up on the sleeping cowboy, Laureline whispered sweetly into her ear, "Samantha Clay, you have a key for a reason."

Sam inhaled sharply, pulling the hat off her face as she sat up, "Laurie!" Blushing furiously as she watched Laureline pocket the hat to wear herself. Sam felt Laureline looked good in everything, especially Sam's clothes. "I waited for you."

Laureline giggled. "I can see that." Kissing her forehead before taking a seat on Sam's lap. "Your hair's gotten longer." Playing with the cowboy's raven strands.

Sam quickly added, "But it don't touch my shoulders." She had promised to come back to Laureline before it grew that long, and a promise to Laureline was more sacred than communion on Sunday.

"Hmmm..." Laureline mused, liking the way Sam's hands felt on her hips, "I feel like this piece is kind of long." Twirling the offending lock around her finger. "How do I know Jed didn't cut some of your hair for you?"

Jaw agape, Sam looked positively mortified, "And be away from you longer?" Shaking her head. "Noooo, this hair is property of Laureline Harper. Ain't nobody touches it but the madam herself." She said, very matter-of-factly.

"Madam?"

"Well ain'cha?"

"What do you mean, Sam?"

"Your hair's like gold and you're soft like velvet. That sounds very madam-like to me."

"Stop messing with those strings, Sam. You're going to undo my whole corset."

"That's the plan," Sam confessed, kissing her neck.

Laureline laughed, a genuine laugh that she'd not had for ages as she swatted at Sam's hands. "Where's Jed?"

"Nevermind Jed." Leading a trail down from Laureline's neck to her collarbone to her rising chest. "He don't need your attention like I do."

"Sam!" Failing to sound at all serious, "Someone might see."

In response, Sam stood up—holding Laureline tenderly in her arms, "Well, I have a key for a reason."

The water felt amazing on her warm skin. As Sam massaged her scalp, Laureline could feel herself sinking deeper into her lover's chest, content to rest in this tub for eternity. "How long are you going to stay in town this time?"

Her question made Sam hesitate. "I dunno, a little while." Bracing for the barrage of follow-ups she knew weren't far behind.

"What's a little while, Samantha?"

"A couple few er so?"

Laureline cocked an eyebrow, "Couple few er so months?"

"Well, no, not month—"

"—You're staying for a few weeks?"

Sam fell silent, reaching over the bath's edge to get the bucket of water sitting on the floor. She poured the warm contents carefully over Laureline's hair, rinsing out the suds. Sam's response was quiet, "Not weeks either."

Laureline turned around in Sam's lap so suddenly that a small wave of water spilled out onto the floor. "How long, Sam?"

Sam was no genius, but it didn't take a genius to know when Laureline was at the end of her patience. Sam tried to take Laureline's hands into her own, but she wasn't having it. "Laurie, please, can I hold you? It's been ages."

"Yeah, Sam, it has been ages. You just got back and now it sounds like you're gonna leave again."

Sam instead placed her hands on Laureline's hips, rubbing Laureline's sides with her thumbs in an attempt to calm her. "I'm not leaving now."

"How. Long. Sam?"

Sam exhaled deeply. "Jed and I leave tomorrow."

Laureline immediately stood up out of the tub, leaving Sam to scramble after her.

"Laurie!"

"Thirteen months, Sam." Snatching the folded towel on the stool and angrily wrapping herself up in it. "You're off chasing bandits and longhorns for over a year and you can only spare me a fucking night? Ha!" Throwing her hands up in the air before going over to her modest wardrobe and yanking out drawers.

Sam left small puddles on the floor as she frantically

followed Laureline across the tiny cabin. "I had to come back, so you could cut my hair."

"Great, so I'm a barber to you." Rolling her eyes as she got dressed.

Sam furrowed her eyebrows, shaking her head in protest. "No, it's not that. I—"

Laureline cut her off, "—No, you just don't think about me until your hair gets too long. Maybe you should just get Jed to cut your hair, you two spend enough time with each other!"

"Laureline Harper!" Sam huffed, her fists glued to her sides as large tears streamed down her face. "That's not fair."

Laureline stared, speechless.

Sam continued, "I'm not learnt like you, Laurie. You know I can't... *talk* fancy and quick like you." She took a moment to find the words, swallowing hard. "Now, I love you, more than anything I've ever known. And you're right, you deserve more than this."

Laureline came closer, hesitating as she reached up to hold Sam's face. Relieved when Sam touched her cheek.

"But two days is all I have right now." Sam whispered.

Laureline searched Sam's eyes, a sadness in her own. "Why? What's going on, Samantha?"

The tension eased, but barely. Sam wrapped her burly arms around Laureline, burying her face in the woman's neck. "It's California—"

"—California? What's that have to do with any of this?"

"I'm getting to that part, let me finish." Planting a kiss on the edge of Laureline's jaw. "There's gold, tons of it."

"How do you know there's gold? Everyone claims there's gold in their backyard."

"Jed and I worked for a man who—"

"—Jesus, Samantha, are you listening to whispers in the wind again?"

"Sweet woman, if you don't stop." Something of a grin pulling at her lips. "We worked for a man, found someone he was looking for. Well that someone happened to be the man's banker. Said the man was rich off several gold mines he'd found in California."

"Why was the man looking for the banker?"

"I dunno, probably because he knew the guy's secret and's been blabbing it to everyone trying to keep from getting caught. That's why Jed and I need to head over to find the gold before someone else does."

The story was not the revelation Sam probably thought it was. Laureline was clearly less than impressed. "You're leaving me for a rumor, Sam."

"I'm not leaving you and it's not a rumor. He showed us papers. If you'd seen that man's house you'd know he was swimming in wealth, more than an acre of tobacco could rationalize. Jed agrees too, and he's smart about these things." Suddenly, Sam fell to her knees, holding onto Laureline's hands as she gazed up at her. "I promise, if I go out there, I'll finally have enough to get you a real plot of land and build a big nice house. You'll have all the fancy dresses you want and you'll never have to worry about nothing ever again, Laurie."

"I never wanted any of those things. I just wanted you, Sam."

The sun had just barely peeked over the horizon but anyone could tell it was a good day to ride.

Jed firmly held the reins of his skittish buckskin overo while looking over to his friend, "You gon' be good?"

Sam's horse was as steady as its rider. She looked back at the small cabin, a small part of her hoping the door would swing open and Laureline would come out, running, but memories of their silent night made quick work of that hope. "Yeah." She cracked her reins and sped off, Jed quickly adding to the banner of dust.By the time their horses had slowed to a gait, hours had passed.

Jed glanced over, all slow and inquisitive-like. He could tell Sam wasn't in the mood for small talk, but Jed never could stand silence. "You know, I think we should look for a nice piano on our way back. Donate it to Clancy's. Anythin'd be better than that run down honky tonk."

Not a word from Sam.

Jed pursed his lips, contemplating. He steered his horse in, close enough to smack Sam on the arm. "I wanted you to ask why."

Sam's eye twitched, "Why what?"

With a *tsk*, Jed continued, "Not like that. Why we should get a piano! Don't you miss hearin' Laureline's singin' voice? And I'm sure she'd be downright tickled to see a genuine ivory. I can practically hear her now." Closing his eyes with a content smile. Though, not even a second later, he sat up straight in his saddle—so as to help hear better. "No, seriously now, I feel like I do hear her..." Looking around.

Sam also scanned their surroundings. Looking behind, she could make out a rider, quickening their pace in approach. "What in tarnation..?"

Calling out to them, Laureline Harper quickly closed the distance, "You two need a third?" Yanking her horse to a halt with a rather accomplished smirk on her face.

"Well I'll be!" Jed smacked Sam's arm once more. "What a pleasant surprise, Ms. Harper. Joinin' us on our journey?"

"No she ain't," Sam asserted.

"Yes I is," Laureline snapped back.

Sam's eyes widened with disbelief, "You ain't never been outside of Louisiana! What did you bring, your entire wardrobe?"

Laureline huffed, "No! I brought the essentials."

Jed leaned over to get a better look at the saddle bag draping over Laureline's horse's backend. "You've got a mighty lot of essentials, ma'am."

"Well, I can't very well wear the same dress the whole time."

Sam and Jed exchanged looks with each other.

"Listen, you two," Laureline jutted a finger out, alternating between both cowboys. "I will never talk to either of you if you don't bring me along. The next time you ride into Millbrooke, I will be gone. Do you understand me?"

Jed burst out laughing; Sam found the threat less amusing. "Oh come on Sam, let's bring her along. What's the worst that could happen? We can protect her from anything the West throws at us."

Flicking the reins of her horse, Laureline trotted past both of them. "I'll remind you both that I handled myself just fine while you two were gone. I don't need none of y'all's protections."

Laureline had never been sicker in her life. She tossed and turned in an attempt to get comfortable. The jacket Sam had laid down for her hardly made the rough dirt any softer, and her movements triggered a nasty coughing fit.

"I ain't never seen nobody this sick before, Sam." Jed murmured, looking on with worry as Sam wiped the beading sweat off Laureline's forehead with the cleanest rag they could find.

Sam breathed a heavy sigh, unsure of what to do. "Whatever she got, she's got it bad, Jed. I don't think we can move her."

Jed crossed his arms. "We crossed the border ages ago. Maybe she got heatstroke from riding so long?"

"I don't think heatstroke makes you cough like that..." Sam touched the side of Laureline's face with the back of her hand. She was burning bad and Sam figured this was one of those doctor's-expert-opinion kind of times. Sam stood. "Dandy's faster than Mister; I'll ride out and bring someone back."

Nodding, Jed walked over to where they'd tied the horses. "Grandean is probably the closest town to us. Not sure if they'll have a doctor though, what with it being so small." He pulled the map out from his saddle bag. "Take this, and if you ain't back in two days, I'm haulin' her myself."

Sam hoisted herself up on Dandy, "It ain't gonna take me two days."

As Sam darted across the sweltering Texas prairie, the surrounding beauty was lost on her. Red mountains, blue wildflowers, and all manner of local creature were not enough to pry her thoughts away from the nauseating feeling building in her stomach. The image of Laureline falling from her horse, how unresponsive she'd been to Sam's panic, played over and over again in her mind. She never should have let her come with them.

When had Laureline first started feeling ill? Why hadn't she said anything? Stubborn, bullheaded woman.

Sam's train of thought was interrupted when Dandy

skidded to a complete stop and reared up with a frightful neigh. Sam pulled hard on the reins, trying to keep in the saddle, "Whoa, Dandy!" Finally losing whatever semblance of control she had and falling off the horse, squarely onto her back, hitting her head.

Dandy was an unbelievably loyal horse. As Sam listened to him flee, she knew whatever had spooked him enough to abandon her must have been bad. She sat up groggily, looking for the source, when suddenly she understood Dandy's sentiments completely.

Before her stood a monster of the devil's own design. Black as night with eyes red like embers. Somehow recognizable as a moth and a man all at once. It was tall, horrifyingly so. Its wings stretched out, casting a nightmarish shadow over Sam. Every instinct she possessed screamed for her to shoot the damn thing, but not a single muscle would obey. Fear had poisoned her.

"You good there, stranger?" An unfamiliar voice offered.

Swallowing hard, Sam blinked, and when her eyes opened, the monster was gone. Instead, a gentleman stood before her, hand outstretched.

She rubbed her eyes furiously, staring back at him absolutely dumbfounded. If it weren't for Dandy's earlier outburst, she would have thought herself mad. "You—but... There was a..." Rubbing the confusion out of her face as she struggled to find the words.

"Not much sure what you mean, but you took a nasty fall from that horse of yours. Should probably get you seen by our doctor-friend here." Gesturing behind him where a sizeable caravan was camped in the near distance.

She cocked a brow. How did she miss an entire convoy? What manner of witchcraft had she stumbled upon? She chanced a glance at the man, catching a glimpse of red in his eyes that vanished when he shielded his face from the sun. A trick of the light, she told herself. And the mysterious camp? A mirage must have hidden it. This was Texas, after all; too much dry heat and all that.

"Come on, I'll help you up." Without her say-so, the man reached down and grabbed her hand, pulling her up to her feet.

Sam had so many questions, skepticisms, and all kinds of bells going off in her head, but finally a thought crawled out of her throat, "You said you got a doctor?"

Jed and Sam rode side-by-side. It was unfortunate about Dandy; Jed knew how loved that horse was. Sam rode Laureline's horse instead.

"So, let me understand this. You lost your good horse."

"Yup."

"Found some frontier dreamers out in the middle of nowhere."

"Yup."

"And they said they'd give us some of their medicine if we helped them get to Oregon?"

"Yup."

"Because they've no protection and they're dog shit at directions."

"Yup."

Jed shook his head, "We ain't actually takin' them to Oregon, are we?"

"Nope."

"Now that's how you get yourself into some trouble, Sam. The universe was kind to you and you're takin' advantage of it."

"We get that California gold, and I'll start sending the universe some kindness of my own."

A third person rode up from the back of the caravan, just in time to interrupt, "Thank you again, fellas. Wouldn't know what to do if you hadn't shown up."

Jed's Southern salesman snuck out, "Happy to oblige! We're a couple a out-west-wanderers ourselves. What're you searchin' for in Oregon, if you don't mind my pryin'?"

The man waved off any notion of being a bother, "Not at all, gentlemen. Many of us are looking for the new heights of adventure." Then he got real quiet, "But as for myself, I'm interested in the mythic folk."

Sam and Jed exchanged one of their knowing looks before Jed continued, "Pardon, mythic folk?" Offering a nervous chuckle.

"Yes, lads! In each of these United States lies a beast of lore and legend. Personally, I'm after the Mothman."

Sam prickled up.

"Mothman? Like a moth that's a man?" Jed inquired. His smile had long faded into disbelief. "Excuse me sayin' so, but I ain't never heard of such a tall tale."

Their third wheel scoffed, "Likely because you boys aren't all that versed in the subject."

Jed relented, "No sir, I reckon we ain't. We're better versed in more useful subjects, like map reading." Managing a curt smirk.

It hadn't been long since the start of their attempt to escort some 23 people from Texas to Oregon. There was an air of disappointment whenever the travelers asked their guides if they'd arrived in the Northeast yet, only to be informed they were still, in fact, in Texas. Much to their dismay, Texas was a lot bigger than they'd anticipated.

Not for Sam and Jed, however. They knew exactly what they'd been in for. In fact, as Laureline's condition slowly improved, they continued their talks of double-crossing.

For the time being, they stopped at Lake Worth, nearly at the heart of the state itself.

Jed addressed the group, "We'll let the horses drink and the youngins can galavant, but everyone keep eyes on each other. We'll leave before long."

As everyone dispersed, Sam took to checking on Laureline. "How're you feeling? Is it too hot back here?" Pushing aside the wagon covers to allow a breeze to drift in.

Laureline smiled weakly. The skin around her eyes was red with sickness, and sweat soaked her blouse. She looked like she wanted to say something, but the words wouldn't come out.

Sam grimaced. "I'ma go get'chu some water, okay?" Hesitating, she eventually departed. The wagon wasn't far from the lake. Its crystal-like waters seemed almost hypnotic, like they demanded reverence.

It was eerie, even. Her gaze drifted over to the left, where a woman lay face down in the water, floating perfectly still. And another oddity: several people at the water's edge seemed to have fallen face first into the sand surrounding the lake, as if paralyzed by their first drink.

Then suddenly, the tranquility of the evening was shattered by a cry, "HELP, SOMEONE, PLEASE!"

All attention was immediately directed toward one of the travelers, a fellow that had kept to himself. His chestnut hair was being plucked out in fistfulls by a creature that bored its mouth into the man's skull. The eyes of its victim were positioned upwards, watching his own consumption as he flailed wildly. It was futile.

Before Sam could lose her insides, she turned away, avoiding the visuals that would have paired with a loud, sickening crunch which silenced the man's pleas for aid. That quiet lasted all of one moment before absolute hell broke loose. Every Oregon-bound individual scrambled to get to their wagons, kicking up dirt, trampling one another, and yelling at the top of their lungs.

And sure enough, the creature gave chase.

Bullets rang out and, much to the horror of those firing them, did nothing to stop the wolf, goat, man-like beast.

Sam made a beeline for Laureline's wagon, avoiding looking at the carnage as if that would somehow keep the monster from noticing her movements. *Forward, forward*, she mentally chanted to herself, involuntarily glancing at the long, serrated jaw of the beast. It shredded the skin off the shoulder of another victim. *Forward.*

She reached the wagon, ripping aside the cover to reveal Laureline, exactly as she'd left her. "Laurie," She started, mind racing a million different ways as she tried to piece together, *what now?* "You stay here, Imma get Jed." She closed the cover, not even processing what the desperate plea Laureline had managed to cough out was.

As soon as Sam turned around, the dauntingness of her task consumed her. There was so much red, Jed could have been in any of it. One thing that was not hard to find, at the center of it all, was the lumbering monstrosity.

Nibbling on the corpses of those unlucky enough to be caught, the lake creature seemed to delight in its wastefulness. Limbs and torsos were strewn in all directions, yet the monster would toss what was already in its mouth and move onto something new, something fresh, something moving.

And all the way over there, on the other side of this hell, was Jed. Laying on his face like the bodies by the lake.

Forward, Samantha.

Lowering herself to a crouch, she skimmed the perimeter. She wasn't going directly for Jed; instead she went for one of the wagon horses, tied to a post. All the others had run off in the initial commotion, but these poor animals were fastened tight with no way of escape. A perfect distraction.

Sam released a pair of horses from the yolk of their wagon before untying them completely and setting them loose. They reared up, much like how Dandy had, neighing and biting before galloping off in different directions.

The creature took the bait. It leapt toward the noise, closing the distance with unfathomable speed and pouncing on one of the horses.

Wasting absolutely no time, Sam sped over into the open and snatched up Jed, straining to pull his dead weight all the way back over to the getaway wagon. There was no time to check for any hopeful signs. Jed was too charismatic to die here and that was enough to steer her on. The distraction's whines died out, but Sam was already shoving Jed's body in next to Laureline.

Who was still alive? No one dumb enough to keep making noise. Sam still needed to get the fuck out of her, so they did what any real, cattle-hardened cowboy would. She untied the horse-drawn wagon from the post, setting it off running with her lover and best friend. Then, as the monster's attention of course moved to its new target, Sam shot it. Again and again and again.

"I told you you'd like California."

Laureline hummed, “Okay okay, you were right. This one time.”

Sam ran her fingers through Laureline’s hair, content to just watch her partner lay on her chest forever. It felt like a dream. “One time’s enough.”

“Well,” wrapping herself closer to Sam, “I think I like it because you’re not going nowhere no more.”

Sam’s fingers trailed down Laureline’s back, watching as she shivered lightly from her touch. “Never again, not without you.”

Laureline repositioned herself, laying completely on top of Sam, “You promise?”

“Laureline Harper, I promise I will not so much as step foot outside this house without your permission.” Something of a grin pulled at Sam’s lips as Laureline inched herself closer for a kiss.

Laureline danced her little finger around Sam’s lips, settling on the new scar that had already healed over. She tilted her head as she spoke, “Is that your attempt at a proposal, Mrs. Cowboy?”

Sam was lost in Laureline, “Well, I do have a key and all.”

SPINWINDER

MATT DWINELL

As far as Bert was concerned, the collective territory of Kansas could kiss his dusty backside. He'd learned to hate this section of the Oregon Trail. Its flat fields that hid gopher holes to twist his ankle in. Its monotonous, dry heat which made his cotton shirt itch. Worst of all, its unpredictable storms.

The threat of one such storm manifested in dark clouds in the distance which had prompted the caravan proper to buckle down the wagons. Unfortunately for Bert, he wasn't proper—caravan or not.

He stood on a little rise about a quarter mile north of the west-ward traveling band. Every manjack of them had to pull their weight, and he'd drawn the short straw for foraging. Bert scoffed, looking down from the rise. There'd been naught to forage here but thorn scratches and broken ankles. The Midwestern sky had turned slate grey, tall grasses waving ominously.

Bert scowled, his short rifle held carelessly in one hand.

With this wind, damn near everything was moving. He wouldn't be catching a rabbit or a deer in this, no way, no how.

Not for the first time, Bert regretted having packed up Molly and the babe and vamoosing out so far from civilization. Civilized folk didn't have to put up with tunnels appearing under their feet, didn't have to make do without bed or stiff drink. There were supposed to be outposts for palaver, trading depots along this stretch. They'd followed in the ruts of previous wagon wheels. Yet the last three depots now—nearly two hundred and fifty miles—had been worse than empty. Buildings blown out like a god had smashed them with his fist.

Giving up seemed the right call here. If not the whole endeavor, then at least the damn northside foraging. He'd tell the group that the game had gone to ground on account of the upcoming weather, which was true enough. Bert munched on the last handful of salmonberries he'd found earlier—those were his secret; didn't he deserve a little something for his efforts? He cast a last cursory glance about the fields.

He squinted. Something was shaping up off near the horizon. Clouds above were spinning up a hell of a conniption fit to the west. Bert cursed. Sure enough, the land had spun up another bum-wad of a disaster.

The twister formed far ahead, its spout reaching for the ground in a way that made Bert think of their babe Martha, grabbing for Molly blindly. Best to prepare to run. This twister was a small one, but that didn't stop it from ripping out scrub and grass, tossing it willy-nilly up into the air. It moved fast too, as ill-fortune tended to.

Bert holstered the gun and got to jogging, heading toward the safety of the wagons. The teams would be anchored, this being no ones' first rodeo against the dirt-sucks of Kansas. He figured he'd make it to the covered wagons in plenty of time;

odds were good that the twister would mosey away from his general direction.

Unfortunately for Bert, this isn't a story about travelers getting lucky.

Dark and downright unfriendly just about described Bert's surroundings as he dashed through the high grass. Seemingly by chance, the twister kept heading generally west, moving erratically until it settled right in between Bert and the caravan.

Bert heard it then, a high-pitched whistling wind, rising in volume as the twister roved closer. He hunted for the nearest streambed. Hell, he'd have tried to stick himself in a rabbit hole if one was nearby. The twister kept between him and the caravan. It moved as if purposeful. Surely that had to be some trick of the mind; no tornado could be controlled.

Bert wedged himself into a creek bed. He hardly noticed the scrapes and scratches and he thanked the sharp rocks where they dug into him, for that meant he was grounded. He even stuck his head down, full flat in the bank, ears submerged and eyes under the water so as nothing could fly into them. This was a moment of peace, sounds of the storm muffled by the creek water in his ears, the stream itself a welcome relief from the region's heat.

It was the last peaceful moment Bert would have.

A howling gale ripped at him, flung water with such force that even head down, Bert's body was jerked about. And the twister still roared and spun, bolstered now with ribbons of water from the stream, its focal point barely twenty feet away. Bert sat up and stared up despite himself. His eyes had to be playing tricks on him again, for it seemed an entire upright tree was in the midst of the spout, not moving. Hard to tell with the wind and debris making it impossible to discern more than an outline.

Bert had just about decided to bolt—to hell with the locals' advice—when the twister pounced. There was no other word for it: One second the maelstrom was as idle as such a devil could be, the next it had Bert fully in its grip.

Bert felt himself ripped from the stream bed. Amid river stones and bits of brushland, he spiraled upward ten feet. Twenty feet. Screaming bloody murder, not that it was audible even to himself over the tearing winds.

Angry air battered him, and he caught another glimpse of some sort of plant in the middle of the twister. Maybe five feet tall, though it was hard to guess when he was upward of twenty in the air and more concerned with dying than some miracle cactus. But he could swear it looked at him. He could swear the thing in the twister realized he was not some bit of brush.

And the darndest thing happened in that second. The winds ceased. The air went utterly still. That blustering force of nature which had thrown Bert like a toddler would a toy abated. Dissipated.

I'm going to die, Bert thought as he plummeted to the ground. Twisting and turning, he landed on his back and legs.

Bert didn't feel much pain at first. Didn't feel much at all. Couldn't much breathe either, though. He gaped at the air uselessly 'cause his lungs had forgotten how to work proper. It had happened before, this fish out of water feeling, air knocked out of him, but it didn't make it any less scary. He turned his head and saw that the plant from earlier had blown apart into a dozen prickly pieces. Felt a flush of confusion at that, and he would have turned back away.

Except.

The ripped-up shreds of this plant weren't still, nor were they moving in the aimless way that wind could toss them either, not a natural wind. Branches and grass stalks, brown and green mottled, they moved. They trembled with purposeful frisson, a thing gathering itself by slow degrees. Storm-scattered roots flexed, snaking toward each other, finding which bits of twigs and tumbleweed connected to which stems.

OhGodohJesusohMaryohFuck. One of his prayers must have been heeded, because Bert drew in a deep shuddering breath. He stood up. Rather, he told his body to do so, but while his lungs had remembered their function, Bert's legs hadn't. His body wouldn't move, didn't have any feeling below the waist.

And before him, one gnarled root joined a spiky protuberance and a few twigs until this prairie plant resembled the lower half of a body; abruptly no longer individual pieces, but legs and feet and more. A hedge-chest scaffolding climbed from a waist of prairie-amalgam.

Bert reached for his gun, but the holster was empty, must have been torn open by the wind. Besides he was afeared that no amount of lead would harm the plant-thing. He began to scream. Wordless, high-pitched. Bert scrabbled backward with his two working limbs tearing at the dirt, ripping off a fingernail in his haste. If he could crawl to the caravan. If he could get out of sight of this thing. If his legs would work. If, if.

The creature finished reassembling itself first. Where a head would be was instead a single tumbleweed spinning in place. It took a step, then another. Not fast steps, but they didn't need to be.

For the first and last time in his life, Bert knew true fear. A fear greater than his own mortality. A fear of the hidden hungers beyond nature, of land best undisturbed, of malice-bound creatures never documented who could rip, and tear, and draw out suffering until death would be a mercy.

The plant-thing reached down and grasped Bert's arm at the point where it had been all scratched up. Insects dove into the wound; plant tendrils grew within his veins. Eventually, Bert knew nothing at all.

It was clear to Molly that her husband wasn't really hers anymore, after the strange twister. Bert spoke in grunts, ate nothing that she could see. A few nights on, she'd caught him looking down at the babe Martha without any expression on his face. She hadn't trusted him since with Martha, or in the wagons at all.

"Some form of battle shock," Pete had told her, nodding in the way men do when trying to convince themselves that they'd pulled wisdom out of their bums. "Happened to a friend of mine back when I was young, after that War of 1812. It'll pass."

Except it hadn't. Six days in, and now they'd called her to a "discussion" about it. Molly sat on a crate in the caravan's vanguard wagon. The trail's ruts jostled her, though far less than the matter at hand.

"Lookie here, were it war neurosis, the dogs wouldn't treat Bert different," Goodie Rogers reasoned. A severe woman whose clothes stayed cleaner than everyone else's. Molly wondered if her lips were stuck in permanent disapproval or if she'd never had reason to change that expression.

Driftwood Jed sucked air between his missing tooth, shook his head. "My hounds ain't attacked him. They're keen is all, pick up on mood changes. The way Bert walks, way he looks at them straight on with that, well, stare. They take it offensive-like is all."

Skip the quartermaster cleared his throat. Molly had always had a soft spot for Skip, perhaps more than was proper if she was telling secrets. He spoke little but got to the point, and always made sure what supplies they had were distributed fairly. "He doesn't eat," Skip spoke. "Not from our supplies."

That struck a chord. If anything Molly had noticed the opposite, and here she said as much. How Bert's bean-pole slim frame had acquired a paunch of late.

The tone of the group grew grim. Hard not to fill, with dark suppositions, the contents of Bert's stomach. Driftwood Jed pointed off in the distance. Ahead of the wagons a speck of dark cloth was all they could see of their guide in a vast landscape of dirt and sky. "Now there's nothing wrong with a bit of the unusual. Think we've all learned not to look a gift horse in the mouth. But there's weird what keeps us out of harm's way, and there's weird that's the harm."

Jed glanced at Molly, and though he spoke gently, it didn't much soften the blow. "With what we've been through this journey, it'd be safest to put Bert down."

Molly clutched the babe to her. She stared down at nothing in particular, hating how a surge of agreement had filled her heart. Bert had his flaws, but for all that he was a good husband. A good man. Didn't he deserve better than to be put down like a hound gone bad? Didn't he deserve another chance? Though her stomach churned at the thought of looking into those horse-dead gentled eyes, Molly spoke. "Give him another week. I'll talk to him then. If anyone's going to put my husband down, it'll be me."

"It isn't proper for—"

"We're a thousand miles west of Proper, Goodie." Molly glared at the woman until the matter was settled.

Another week passed. Molly couldn't help but notice the little details. Changes, subtle and not, were taking place in Bert. The man looked to be surviving but not living. He hadn't washed his clothes. The denim jacket he took such pride in was in shambles, his Stetson hat long since blown away. The top of Bert's thinning head had gotten deeply sunburnt; it was a common sight for any looking back, as he followed behind the caravan with an increasingly stooped gait. Ask him a question, and he'd grunt, shy away.

They'd passed another trading depot. This fourth location was also deserted and destroyed. No palaver, no supplies. Only a keening wind that whistled around a single still-standing wall, and the tracks of uprooted foliage from some beast Molly didn't want to think about.

"He'll come back to us," she'd said. Molly knew in her heart of hearts that she and the babe would be safest if he didn't. If Bert up and absquatulated off into the Kansas fields and never returned. Because a broken man was dangerous, like a jagged edge of glass. The nearer he was kept, the more likely you'd be cut.

On the fifth day, as evening wound down and the distant howls of coyotes made a nighttime chorus, Molly passed Martha to Goodie. Goodie, for all she was made of rattlesnake venom and spite, had raised three strong sons well enough that they'd left her house soon as emancipated. The babe would be safe with her for a few hours. Before Molly confronted Bert, she rapped softly at Driftwood Jed's wagon and begged for his army-issue piece. *For wild varmints,* she lied to herself.

She strode a few steps in the direction they'd come, then waited as night fell. Kansas had a wild beauty to it. It stirred at Molly in the quiet moments. Moments of perfect weather and clear skies that tempted her to run through fields for the sheer joy of it.

This night, lulled by the nearby susurrus of prairie

insects and the far-away cries of coyotes, it made her wish for a fire to warm her without and a bit of stiff drink for within. Made her consider raising a kid in the middle of all this nature. Made her wonder if they needed to journey full chisel to Oregon when there was plenty unclaimed for them here.

Bert lurched out of that perfect night. She saw him coming from across the hill. Half-clouded moonlight caught him on his back, showing enough that something looked wrong, but not enough to show him human. He stopped maybe fifteen feet afore her, feet shuffling uncertainly.

"Bert," she tried. The man who had once been her husband grunted. Raspy and dry, was it just a trick of the wind or had his sounds gotten quieter?

"Bert, they're worried about you. I'm worried about you." With the solid heft of Jed's piece at her hip, Molly could admit *I'm worried* of *you*. Again, Bert only grunted.

"Bertie. Listen to me. Give me a sign that you're in there. How about this, then. You don't got to speak. Make one noise for no, and two for yes. How 'bout that? Can you do that for me?"

A blast of wind blew at Molly's dress, spat dust in her face so she blinked and rubbed her eyes. When the dust cleared, Bert swayed back and forth almost in arm's reach. She grabbed the pistol. Bert grunted, swayed, grunted again.

Two grunts meant yes, or was that sheer happenstance?

Speaking slowly so as not to spook a wild animal, Molly asked "Bert, do you understand me?" Two more grunts. She could work with grunts. He seemed to focus sharper too, whenever she used his name. "Bertie, can I help you?"

One grunt. Her eyes had adjusted to the night now and it showed how while Bert swayed, he kept his own eyes on the ground. Ashamed, mayhap. Embarrassed.

"Bert, is there anything that can make this better?" Two grunts, and why did that break her heart so?

"Food?" No. "Water?" No. "Any medicine?" No.

"Bertie dear, this could take all night. Do you know what it is you need?" Two grunts, yes. Another breeze tickled the hem of her skirt.

"Give me a sign if you can, Bertie. Show me."

She thought she'd pushed him too far. He stood there for a moment with all the wit of a sleeping cow. He raised one shaking arm. His fingers pointed to her. No, not to her, but her hip and the gun holstered there.

"Bert, no. There's got to be another way, dear. We can work through this." Like they'd fallen into marital problems. Like this was some picayune squabble they could logic their way out of.

The cloudcover over the moon passed, and Molly's words died in her throat. There would be no working through this. Bert's arm wasn't shaking. That was the effect of thousands of tiny insects walking up and down the limb. Bert's face on hers, now that she could see, wasn't just hard-off. The prairie dust hid the fact that the skin was tearing, that a section of naked jawbone jutted exposed. He met her eyes for that second, and for once there was a spark of emotion. A crinkling of eyebrows, a worried crease in the forehead, a glassy eyed sheen of sorrow.

She reached for him.

And Bert's left eye fell out.

From the gap came a questing tendril, mottled brown and green. It moved hesitantly. Molly didn't. She sank all six bullets into Bert's torso. Clicked the gun uselessly once it was out, as if it'd reload from prayer alone. Besides jerking at the impact, Bert only seemed angry. Molly turned—loathe as she was to lose sight of what Bert had become, lest it reach her—and sprinted back to the dubious shelter of the camp.

~

"You did the right..." Goodie trailed off after seeing what must have been on Molly's face. Molly stared round the fire, saw everyone tense and unsure. From behind, a keening wind was growing, buffeting now at the wagons, whipping the fire towards frenzy. They looked around.

"We have a situation. Like that devilry in the sinkholes. Like what happened by that lake. Bert's..."

"How many of them bullets did you hit him with, you think?" Jed asked.

"All of them. Point blank. He's something else now—we ought to run!"

"Wind's picking up. No time." Skip nodded slow, as if to contradict his statement, like her cold-as-a-wagon-tire husband wasn't coming to pay a visit right this second. "Reckon we fight."

Men with hard faces and women with makeshift weapons from the camp. Even children, pulling out slings and pouches filled with well-worn pebbles. Molly shook her head at them. "Six bullets or sixty, it won't matter."

A shape entered the firelight. It flitted in stutter-quick steps, a dark trench coat flapping behind it. Seven foot tall if it was an inch. Molly's hand grabbed for the spent pistol, and she wasn't the only one twitchy, but this shape had come from the west. Red eyes in a black cloak, the caravan's guide didn't quite come into full view. He shifted from one boot-clad foot to the other. Then, once all eyes were on him, their guide threw a branch into the fire. Wet, it crackled and sizzled, before falling to the wind-whipped flames.

Molly needed no more prompting. "We burn the bastards that've taken my husband," she declared.

"With this wind, we're like to cause a blaze which could eat up the wagons and keep going," Jed protested. But half a chance beat none at all. Folk grabbed spare sticks, wrapped whatever was on hand that would burn around the edges. They swathed the ends of the sticks with oil and rags, pressed them into the fire and turned to the east.

In the flickering firelight, her fellow traveler's faces were cast into half shadow, harsh red orange highlighting half their visage. Simon and Milo and Otto, folk who'd not shy from what must be done. Molly took comfort in how little fear showed on their faces. Even Goodie looked like to scold this plant thing until it collapsed. *If Goodie's here, who's taking care of the babe?*

Before she could ask, poor Bert shambled toward them. Well, what had once been Bert. It didn't stop or hesitate this time. Instead, Bert screeched. A keening wail poured out of him, and the time for thought was over.

Flash of makeshift torch. Jabbing, adrenaline making her arms strong. Wind whipping smoke, embers blowing into her face. Leaves and grass spinning, spiraling upward. Driftwood Jed snarling, running forward. Jed's legs still pumping midair as gusts of wind tossed him like a ragdoll. Screaming and hollering. Skip's voice raised above it all: "Can't throw all of us at once, surround it." She ran in on some instinctive cue, hunched over. Felt the pressure as her fire stick connected to Bert. So much less resistance than she'd expected. His skin tore easy as parchment, spilling bugs and green bundles. The gale knocked her onto her back, catching her elbows. She saw saw

Bert afire. In that moment it was clear to all, Molly and Jed and those who'd passed off the previous problems as a trick of the light, that this was not Bert. Bert was long dead, and the twisted immolating scarecrow before them was not of nature but of Nature.

It commanded them to fear. The keening shriek had

become a gale around it, spinning, a twister in its own right which obscured the cursed contents within. There was a second where Molly could have sworn that she saw two red glowing eyes above the twister. Beholding all below, but not interfering.

And then the winds slowed, the twister exfluncticated before it properly connected sky to ground, a stillborn birth. And birth it would have been. For as the winds cleared, the seed pods of a plant they'd no record of lay scattered along the ground.

It was a somber crew who cleaned them up, setting each bundle to burn. Molly couldn't shake the feeling that she was killing Bert all over again with each seed she destroyed. The pods held movement sometimes, at the beginning. Strange insects fled before the heat, and the seeds themselves beat to the peristalsis of some unseen heart.

The caravan crew linked arms, made a horizontal line and walked, scoured the area for all the seed that night. They did it all over again the next morning, bolstered by sunlight and anti-fogmatic that Skip rationed out for the occasion. Molly had grown rather numb by the end of the ordeal, and eventually someone passed the babe back into her arms. Jed and Skip were talking nearby as everyone prepared to leave. Mostly Jed talked and Skip nodded sagely, as was typical of Skip and anyone else conversing.

"I mean, Bert—the thing that took him over—must've destroyed the trading posts, right? Great big monster tracks, torn up ground, tossed houses?"

Skip nodded.

"You think there are more of those things out there? Could be we missed one of those seeds from last night."

Skip shrugged.

"Yeah... Yeah, I don't much like the thought of staying here any longer than it takes to piss. You got a top-off for my flask?"

Skip nodded, offered a wan smile.

Molly rocked Martha and tried to blink away the events of the night before. The babe had some toy clutched tight in her little hands, probably small enough to put in her mouth.

"Drop it," Molly cajoled, holding out a bit of real food instead. Martha shook her head. "Da-Da," the babe said instead. Molly worked at the babe's closed fist and pried it open. In her daughter's hands rested a bright green seed pod.

Molly ripped it away, ignoring the wails, and stomped it into the dirt. She called out for tinder and a bit of that whiskey.

She prayed there hadn't been another one that the babe had already gotten her hands on.

Sometime later, their guide resumed wandering westward. The sojourners followed as best they could.

SHUNKA WARA'KIN

DAVID BADENCHINI

The beautiful forests and open plains were contrasted by the brutally hot sun that beat down on Cyrus' brow. He removed his hat, wiped his forehead with his sleeve, and put it back on for the twenty-fifth time today. At least he didn't have to work too hard as he rode. His horse's presence was usually enough to keep the livestock in line. When the occasional sheep was going too slow, he didn't even have to whip it; Spot did all the work for him.

"Cyrus!" Lemuel's horse rode up. "My pa says we'll be setting up camp soon."

"Thank goodness. How was your herding today?"

"It was awful. Fido won't listen to me at all. I nearly wore my arm out with cracking the whip. He's nothin' like your Spot there." Lemuel looked ahead to see Spot nipping on the heel of a sheep that went too far from the rest of the herd. It immediately ran to join the others.

"Spot makes this easy for me. I can't deny it."

"Hold on. Is that a cabin up ahead?"

Lemuel pointed. It was hard for Cyrus to see since the sun

was close to setting, and it shone straight into his eyes. But he could see the walls of a log cabin peaking over the grassy hill-side. Surrounded by pine trees, it sat right on the edge of the woods on the northside of the trail.

The wagons slowed. People were getting out and rounding up the animals. Cyrus and Lemuel dismounted from their horses.

Lemuel spoke absent-mindedly to himself, saying, "There better not be another goddamned goat-thing in these woods." He winced as he looked up to Cyrus and said, "Uhh, don't tell my pa I said that."

Spot ran up to Cyrus, who leaned down and scratched behind his ears. "Good work today, boy! You earned yourself an extra helping of dinner."

It wasn't until after sunset that dinner was ready. One of the women of the caravan filled up bowls with stew from the large cauldron that sat over the campfire. Cyrus sat beside Lemuel and Jemima as they ate. Spot rested on his lap, and Cyrus couldn't help but occasionally fish out a piece of buffalo meat to give to him.

Nearly the whole caravan was sitting directly on the grassy dirt around the fire. Horace, one of the older men and the unofficial leader of the caravan, was standing by a fella who Cyrus had never seen before. Horace addressed everyone present as he spoke. "This here is Obadiah. He lives in that tiny cabin there. He agreed to let us camp here on his land, so I want everyone to be polite and welcoming to him. And make sure he has his fill of the stew."

"It's no trouble," Obadiah said. "I'm happy to see some new faces. It gets awfully lonely in that cabin all by myself." He took a bowl of stew and ate a bite before continuing. "You see, my profession of choice is that of a storyteller. Can I interest you all in a tale?"

Several voices from the caravan encouraged him to continue. "Alrighty then. Well, I used to be on a caravan of my own a long time ago. We were on the Oregon Trail, but got a bit lost. Hence why we got so far north. I imagine you all are in a similar situation. As we were travelin', we came across..."

"Cyrus," Lemuel whispered. "Have you seen Fido?"

"Fido? No," said Cyrus. "I thought you were with him all day."

"I was, but I haven't seen him in an hour or so. Must've wandered off somewhere."

"Uh-oh! Looks like you lost him!" teased Jemima. "What's your pa gonna say when he finds out?"

"Shit. I'd better go looking for him then." Lemuel finished his stew in a few quick gulps, then got up and walked away from the group.

"...way too much buffalo for us to take with us. So we decided to just set up camp here until we finished eating it all!" Obadiah's story got a laugh from most of the crowd.

"But little did we know that these parts were occupied by a *terrible beast!"* He exaggerated the last two words, inducing a frightful squeal from the children.

"The natives call it the Shunka Wara'kin. It's some kind of giant wolf. Like if a wolf and a bear had a baby. I've seen it with my own eyes!"

As if on cue, a howl was heard from the nearby forest. Cyrus had seen and heard wolves before, but they never sounded anything like this. The bestial sound coming from the woods was eerie and unnatural.

"I'm tellin' you, that was it! There ain't no wolves around here. Just the beast. Now, me and my brother and his family—

we didn't know there was such a beast in these parts. Not until we realized that one of us was missing. No matter where we looked, we couldn't find Jip. We stayed campin' here for an extra day, but there was still no sign o' him.

"My brother wanted to keep on movin'. But I wanted to stay; I couldn't leave ol' Jip behind! You see, my brother had 'is family to worry about. His wife, his kids. Ain't no way was he about to stay around 'ere any longer for any old dog!"

"Oh. Okay, I get it now," Jemima whispered. "I was thinkin' that 'Jip' was a weird name, but I guess not for a hound."

"My brother and I couldn't agree, so he left and took his family with him. But I stayed. I camped and hunted on my own. I even started a garden, and I traded for goods from those who'd pass by on the trail. And all the while, I kept on lookin' for Jip.

"Eventually, I began to notice that whenever travelers would come through here, they'd usually mention that one o' their dogs had gone missing. So one night, I stayed up late and kept watch. That was when I saw it. Not Jip, no. I saw *it.* The beast. The Shunka Wara'kin itself!

"Apparently, it has a tendency to steal dogs away from people. I swear on my own two eyes, it ran right past a herd of helpless cattle just to grab one of the dogs. It bit onto its neck, and dragged it into the woods. It doesn't seem to kill 'em, so I'm not so sure why it does it. Maybe it's just lonely. Maybe it had a pack of its own once, so now it wants other dogs to keep it company. Having lived here alone for all this time, I can almost relate.

"Well, anyway, I eventually came to enjoy my solitary life here. I built myself a cabin, and I've been livin' off the land ever since. And now I do my best to give a fair warning to any other travelers. Watch your dogs, else they get taken in the night like mine was!"

Cyrus was running through a forest that he didn't recognize. He was frantic, though he didn't know why. Suddenly, he heard a scream. There was no mistaking it. It was her. "Ma! Where are you?!"

He turned around a tree just in time to see it. The earth opened up beneath her, and she fell into a deep hole. Cyrus looked inside the bottomless pit. She was gone. He was just as powerless as the first time.

Cyrus heard the bleating of a goat. He turned around, already knowing what was behind him. The goat-man towered over him. "Cyrus, run!" His father jumped in front of him, and valiantly charged at the monster.

Cyrus tried to warn him. He tried to shout, but no words could escape his throat. The goat-man charged into his father, launching him into a tree. His neck snapped on impact. The monster then turned its attention toward Cyrus.

Cyrus suddenly awoke. It wasn't a goat-man that was there, but a dog. Spot was pawing at him and nuzzling him, whimpering the whole while.

"It's okay boy, I'm fine! It was just a bad dream." He held Spot close and scratched him behind the ear. Spot was always there to comfort him when he needed it.

In just the past few months, the caravan had had more than a few frightening encounters with creatures and phenomena that no one could explain. Everyone wanted to pretend that it hadn't happened, but Cyrus felt the pain of being without his parents every day. Spot was the only one he had left who could make him feel like he wasn't alone.

Cyrus tried to go back to sleep, but it wasn't long before he heard a voice outside his tent. "Cyrus, are you asleep? Wake up."

"What is it, Lemuel?"

"I can't find Fido. I need your help searchin' for him."

Cyrus sighed. "Alright, fine. Let's get lookin'."

He exited his tent, and he and Lemuel split up to cover more ground. The whole caravan was asleep, so he was sure to be quiet. After searching for an hour, Cyrus had nearly given up when he saw Lemuel approaching in the moonlight. A dog was following closely behind him.

"So you found 'im?"

"No," Lemuel said. "This is Nellie, Jemima's dog. I was fooled too with how dark it is."

"Well, I'm not sure what to do at this point," Cyrus said. "I've looked everywhere."

"Wait!" Lemuel pointed out towards the treeline at the edge of the forest. "Is that him?"

Sure enough, there was a silhouette of a hound standing by the trees. "I'll go get him. You just take Nellie back." Cyrus approached the trees.

As he got closer, Cyrus was surprised to see how big Fido seemed. *Is it a trick of the light? It has to be. Obadiah said there were no wolves around here.*

It wasn't until Cyrus was a mere fifty feet away that he heard a growl unlike anything he'd ever heard before. He froze. This wasn't Fido. It had matted, wild fur, disproportionately large front legs, and a jaw larger than a bear's. Its eyes shone a sickening yellow in the moonlight.

No. It's real?! Cyrus began to back up slowly, but the beast was approaching him. Its growling was growing louder. It looked like it was about to pounce.

Cyrus turned and ran, but he could hear it following

behind. It was gaining on him. He looked over his shoulder, but regretted it. The huge, snapping jaws nearly had him.

Suddenly, another source of barking came out from the night. A much smaller shape beelined towards the monster. It heroically bit onto its neck, stopping it in its tracks.

"Spot! Get back!"

The Shunka Wara'kin tried to shake Spot off, but he kept holding on. It wasn't until it lifted up its massive paw and swiped at Spot that he let go. It placed the heavy paw atop Spot, pinning him to the ground.

Cyrus turned to see the monster looming over Spot. His dog couldn't get away. "Stop! Let him go!"

All the fear that had driven Cyrus to run away was gone, and a new fear now prompted him to sprint directly at the beast. He was about to lose something far more important than his life. He screamed loud enough to surely wake up the entire camp.

"Give him back!"

The Shunka Wara'kin bit onto Spot's neck. It turned away and began to drag him into the forest. The monster moved too quickly. Cyrus sprinted faster than he'd ever thought he could, but it wasn't enough. Even dragging Spot along with it, it was still getting away. Spot kept squirming and yelping the whole time, but there was nothing he could do to escape the beast's jaws.

By the time Cyrus reached the treeline, they were both long gone. Spot's yelps were getting quieter and quieter. Cyrus fell to the ground in despair. *What am I supposed to do now?*

"Alright, looks like we're all saddled up! Make sure you didn't leave anything behind. We gotta get a move on. Sun's been up for an hour, and daylight's a-wastin'!"

Horace continued barking orders, making sure that the caravan was ready to move out. He took his seat in the box of the head wagon. Taking hold of the reins, he raised his whip to stir the oxen into motion, but he stopped as he saw Cyrus approaching at a full sprint.

"Cyrus!" he bellowed. "Why ain't you at the back of the caravan on your horse? I need you to keep the cattle in line."

Cyrus' speech was interrupted by his heavy panting, like he couldn't afford to simply catch his breath first, else it'd be too late. "We can't... leave yet... I still... haven't found... Spot..."

"Spot? Your dog? If you lost 'im, son, then I guess it'll just be a hard day for you. Get ready to put that whip to use, and get back to your horse already!"

"No! We can't leave. We can't leave Spot behind."

Wood creaked as Horace stood from his seat before dropping to the ground. He stood tall over Cyrus. He was not one to have his orders questioned, especially not by a youth.

"Look me in the eyes, boy. If you lost your dog, that's your mistake. Find yourself another one at our next stop, or hope that Jemima's dog Nellie births some more pups. But we ain't waitin' here any longer to fix your mistake. Now get on your goddamned horse, or you're gettin' left behind!"

Cyrus had always been too scared to stand up to Horace. Everyone was. The man's scolding in this moment was nearly enough to make Cyrus fold and do as he was told. But he would never abandon Spot.

He looked up at him with a fiery determination. "If I gotta stay, I'll stay. But I ain't leavin' without Spot."

Horace glared down at him. Cyrus began to imagine the worst. Would Horace beat him senseless, then throw him into a wagon and take him with them despite his wishes? But much to his surprise, Horace's response wasn't a fraction as aggressive as he expected.

"...Fine. We'll stay for one more day, son. Only one day. If you haven't found your dog by then, that's on you."

Cyrus marched alone through the woods. He had tried to follow the monster's trail, but he wasn't good enough at tracking. He kept losing the trail, finding it again, and ended up going in a circle. He held a rifle that he borrowed from one of the caravan wagons. No way Horace or anyone would have given it to him freely. But he needed it regardless. He wanted to kill the monster so it could never steal another dog again.

He froze as he heard the sound of stirring leaves behind him. He turned, raising the rifle. "Hold it!" said the man. "It's just me. I ain't no wild beast."

It was Obadiah. He was approaching from a distance away, and he also had a rifle slung across his back. "Your people mentioned you were lookin' for your dog. Is that right?"

Cyrus nodded. "Spot. I didn't believe your story at first. But I saw the monster take him. I have to get him back."

"I understand, son. The same thing happened to me. I still miss ol' Jip."

"You've been here for a long time. Did you ever find where that thing lives or where it may've taken Spot?"

Obadiah nodded slowly. "I never quite found whatever den it calls home, but I've tracked it many times. All the tracks lead to the northern region of the forest. That's the best place to start lookin'."

Cyrus responded enthusiastically. "That's great, mister! Would you show me the way?"

"Well," Obadiah answered hesitantly. "I can. But I'm not

sure if I should. That thing's a wild animal, son. It's dangerous. You should head on back to your people."

"But you said it only snatches up dogs. It doesn't hunt humans."

"Neither do wolves or bears, but they'll still kill a man if he trespasses on their territory. Listen, I understand how hard this must be for you, but this is just unwise. I give you my word that I'll go lookin' for your dog and I'll bring him back to you if I can find 'im. But you should leave the forest and just wait for me to get back. You're young. Don't go throwin' your life away."

A man strode down a dirt road, carrying a tall stack of crates in his arms. Finally arriving at his destination, he placed the crates down on the ground outside of a humble cabin. He caught his breath and wiped his brow. Outside the structure, a woman and a young boy were loading their belongings into a wagon. The woman approached and picked up the top crate which was full of linens.

"These are great, honey! They will do us well for the journey."

"Let's hope it's enough," the man replied. "That was the last of the money we'd saved." He bent down and picked up the remaining stack of crates again.

They sauntered over to the wagon and began looking for room to fit the boxes. The young boy looked up at the man and spoke. "Why do we need all this stuff, Pa?"

"Because, Cyrus, we're going somewhere far away. We need to be ready to travel for a long time."

"Why don't we stay here?"

The man picked up a crate full of bread and vegetables and

placed it on the wagon. "There isn't enough food, money, or land here for everyone. So we're going west. They say there's enough gold for everyone out there!"

"Am I goin' too?" asked the boy.

"Of course, son! We're a family, and family has got to stick together."

The boy looked down. He was apprehensive. This was a big change for him, and he was clearly scared. The man bent down on one knee and placed a reassuring hand on the boy's shoulder.

"Don't fret, Cyrus. Family sticks together, and so long as we have each other, everything's gonna be alright."

The boy nodded, not fully convinced. "Are my friends coming too?"

The man sighed. "Some of 'em. Several other families are joinin' the trek, but not everyone."

The boy looked sullen again.

The man reached down to a crate of potatoes and took hold of it. "Well, I know there's no replacing your friends, Cyrus. But I figured it'd help if I got you a new friend before we headed on our journey."

He lifted the potato crate, revealing the content of the last crate underneath. Inside was a squirming bundle of white fur speckled in black spots. It instantly leaped from the box onto the boy, and the puppy began to eagerly lick his face. The boy squealed with joy, unable to contain his laughter.

"Now, you'll take good care of 'im, won't you Cyrus?"

"I will, Pa! I promise. You can count on me!"

"He's the only family I got left. I ain't goin' back without him."

Obadiah wasn't surprised by Cyrus' answer. He opened his

mouth to retort, but the boy's expression left him lost for words. The youth was deadset on this path.

"Alright," Obadiah sighed. "If you want to come, I can't stop you. Just let me lead the way, and keep that gun at the ready."

Obadiah guided Cyrus deeper into the forest. The terrain was rough. There was no path to follow, seeing how there was no human foot traffic through this region. There was no conversation between them, and the only sounds to accompany them were the crunching of leaves and the chirping of the birds and squirrels.

Cyrus was attentive as they walked, looking for any signs of Spot or his captor. As the day dragged on, Cyrus began to grow tired, and Obadiah's pace slowed a little. Through the leaves overhead, he could see that the sun was moving. Hours were going by, and they still hadn't even reached the monster's territory.

And once we get there, we'll have to search for its den. Even Obadiah had never found it. How am I gonna find Spot in time at this rate? By the time I get back, will the caravan have already left? Lord, help me.

Sure enough, the hours dragged on, and the sky began to darken. "Are we in the beast's territory yet, Obadiah?" Cyrus asked.

"Not yet," Obadiah said. "It should still be about two hours in this direction."

"Two hours! It'll be dark by then. I don't have time for this, gran'pa! I need to bring Spot back before my people leave me."

Obadiah turned to him. "If you're so worried, you can head on back right now. Let me handle findin' your dog."

"I can't!" Cyrus said. "There's gotta be a way to find it. Somethin' we're missing..."

"I know what I'm doin', son. There are more of that creature's tracks down this way than I've ever seen. It's gotta live in this direction."

Cyrus looked around. After finding a suitable tree, he began to climb it, then stopped about twenty feet up. He used the vantage point to continue surveying the area. "Look!" he shouted. "Over that way! I think I see some tracks."

He jumped down, then ran to the spot he'd seen. Sure enough, there were large pawprints in the mud. They were the size of a bear's paw, yet looked different than any print Cyrus had seen before.

"That's the wrong way," Obadiah said.

Cyrus continued to follow the trail for a few more feet. "I don't think so. These prints are fresh."

"That don't mean nothin', son. Those tracks lead eastward. Its territory's to the north."

Cyrus paused. He bent down closer to the ground. "Obadiah! There's some droplets of dried blood here! That thing was bitin' Spot on the neck. They had to have gone this way!"

Obadiah approached and looked at the droplets that littered the earth. "Well goddamned. So that's why I could never find its den. I've been overshootin' it all this time. Just 'cause there's more tracks down that other way don't mean it necessarily lives there I suppose."

Cyrus eagerly began to follow the trail, and Obadiah did his best to keep up. It took less than an hour for them to reach their destination: the entrance to a cave that went into the side of a hill.

"Let's go. The sun's setting. We ought to hurry," Cyrus said. He strode toward the cave's entrance.

"Now hold on," Obadiah said. "Goin' into the Shunka Wara'kin's den? That's insane! It's a wild beast, 'n you want to back it into a corner? Let's just wait out here for it to come out."

Cyrus continued his approach until he came to a sudden stop at the cave's entrance. Obadiah followed behind, and he saw what had given Cyrus pause. Just within the entrance, there lay the remains of a fresh carcass. The flesh was in ribbons, and it was little more than a pile of entrails, broken bones, and torn hide.

It was undeniably a dog.

Obadiah broke the silence. "Is that—?"

"No. It's not Spot. But poor Lemuel isn't gonna be happy to hear what happened to Fido." He turned to look at Obadiah. "I guess you were wrong about the beast not killing the dogs it takes. It just likes to take them home first."

"Son. It's time we head back."

Cyrus' expression was blank. He said nothing as he slowly turned and began to march into the cave.

"Cyrus!" Obadiah called. "Spot must be long gone by now. There's no point to this anymore!"

Cyrus felt empty, devoid of both hope and despair. He didn't know why his body was moving. Was he still striving to rescue his dog, or to simply avenge him? He couldn't decide, and he didn't care to. He held his rifle out in front of him as he continued alone into the darkness.

The scent of raw meat and fresh entrails wafted through the air as Cyrus stepped past Fido's corpse. He couldn't let this happen again. Not to any other dog. Not to Spot. He'd end this tonight.

He continued deeper into the darkness. His lantern was hanging by a short rope that looped around his wrist as he held the rifle in both hands. As if on cue, a sudden boom of thunder preceded a rainfall that quickly became heavy and loud. Cyrus turned to the cave's entrance, and for a moment he thought he saw glowing red eyes perched on a large tree branch barely visible through the gloom. It was gone with the next lightning strike, and Cyrus concluded that it must have been an owl. Echoes of the storm reverberated through the cave, and a stream began to pour into it as Cyrus strode deeper into the earth.

He was soon met by the sight of the beast's leftovers. More corpses of both wolves and dogs, each of them being a past meal. Very few of them had any wet flesh left on them, and all of them smelled of rot. How many dogs had this thing killed? Why would a creature so similar to a wolf eat its own kind with such fervor? Cyrus pondered this for the briefest moment before realizing that he didn't particularly care. He only wanted to make it stop.

Progressing further, Cyrus soon found a steep, vertical drop. It went down about twelve feet with the cave continuing past it. Deep claw marks on the stone showed that the monster consistently used this path. It was apparently quite good at climbing.

At first, Cyrus was hopeful that he'd find Spot near the cave's entrance, as he thought that Spot would be trying to escape, assuming he was alive. Cyrus saw it as a bad sign that he didn't encounter Spot in the first few minutes. But this short cliff gave him an ounce of optimism. It was too steep for any normal canine to climb, so it was no wonder Spot wasn't able to escape. Cyrus painstakingly climbed down, using the slick rocks as handholds. He barely managed to get to the bottom without losing his grip. He knew he wouldn't be able to get out fast enough to escape, but he didn't care. This would only end with either him or his quarry dead.

The cave opened up into a larger chamber. All the dog corpses here were collected into a single, large pile, and several branching tunnels extended to both the left and right. Cyrus began to circle the pile of dog bones as he peered into various passageways; he needed to choose where to explore first. But which way would he find Spot? He could call for him, but the monster would surely hear. Should he do it anyway? Did he *want* to encounter the creature right now?

Well, thought Cyrus, *I am going to kill it today. I might as well.* He took a deep breath, but before he could start shouting, there was a loud sound of rustling and movement behind him. He turned to see a large mass rising out from the pile of dog corpses in the center of the room. Bones shifted and poured across the stone floor as the monster raised its head to look at Cyrus. Then the bones cracked and crunched beneath its weight as it stepped forward.

The Shunka Wara'kin's eyes gleamed in the lantern light. Its otherworldly growl echoed through the chamber. Cyrus aimed his musket. He was at point blank range, yet his arms quaked. *I can't afford to miss,* he thought. *I'll let it take two more steps forwards, then shoot.*

It placed one paw onto the cold stone beyond its nest of bones. Its teeth were bared. Its breathing was both heavy and raspy. It crouched slightly lower as it raised its other paw to step closer.

One more step...

In a flash, it lunged. The mass of fur and fangs was directly before Cyrus. He fired.

Bang!

The creature's mass collided with him, and Cyrus found himself slammed into the ground. The creature's weight pinned him down, but thankfully, it was still. Cyrus' rifle was halfway in its mouth, and a new hole had been made at the back of its neck. After taking a second to catch his breath, Cyrus slowly wriggled his way out from under the monster.

"Spot!" he shouted. "Spot, are you here?!"

There was no answer. No noise. No sign that there was anything else alive down here. Cyrus' anxiety rose in a matter of seconds. He started heading toward the mouth of one of the branching tunnels. Then, he finally heard a noise.

The Shunka Wara'kin had shakily raised itself back to its feet.

No.

It pointed its snout in Cyrus' direction. Then began to approach. Cyrus backed up until he hit the wall. He was standing at the base of the vertical drop. He knew he wouldn't be able to climb it quickly enough. He was cornered.

The beast's steps were wobbly and unstable, yet its sheer size was enough that it would still be able to kill Cyrus with ease. Its mouth hung open, and blood poured out continuously.

It should be dead. This thing isn't natural. I'm gonna be killed by a demon!

There was no getting away. Cyrus had put the rifle down, and it had only one shot anyway. He didn't have the time or supplies to reload it. The demonic wolf loomed before him, growling like thunder, before it suddenly cut off and it turned away with a yelp. Behind the monster, with its teeth clamped onto its tail, was Spot!

The beast thrashed about, spinning this way and that. But it couldn't reach Spot. As it chased its own tail, it lost its balance and fell to the ground, before picking itself up again and continuing. Finally, it came to an end as the beast turned quickly enough that Spot was flung into the stone wall. But it only had a moment to regain its bearings before Spot leaped at it, biting onto the monster's ear.

Despite all his ferocity, Spot was slapped aside. The beast pinned him down with a heavy paw. Cyrus shook himself from his surprise, and quickly found a large rock on the ground. Lifting it over his head with two hands, he charged the creature.

Bang!

The Shunka Wara'kin slumped to the ground before Cyrus could even reach it. Blood poured out of a wound on its side. Cyrus dropped the stone and kept running, shoving the beast off of Spot. And he was greeted with a wet nose and many licks.

"Spot! I knew I'd get you back! It's okay! You're gonna be alright, boy!" He hugged Spot and cried and laughed with joy.

"Well I'll be," Obadiah spoke. "I didn't think there was a hope."

Cyrus looked up to where Obadiah sat at the top of the vertical segment of the cave. Smoke still trailed off the end of his rifle.

"Obadiah!" he called. "You *did* come. Thank you."

He gave a humble nod. "I couldn't save ol' Jip. But if I could save one fella's hound, then I'd say that my time livin' out here was well worth it."

Cyrus climbed the rope that Obadiah lowered after hoisting Spot up. He took one last look at the Shunka Wara'kin. Was it really dead? It wasn't moving. Cyrus decided it'd be best to move quickly and hope they wouldn't have to find out.

Before long, Cyrus, Obadiah, and Spot were leaving the cave and making their way back. But they didn't get too far before Spot suddenly tensed. He looked back in the direction of the cave and bared his teeth. Cyrus and Obadiah looked on in silence before a pained howl reached their ears.

"Why won't it die?" Cyrus whispered.

"I don't know, son. Lord help us."

The Shunka Wara'kin sprinted out of the cave. Its limbs were moving in a haphazard mess, head flailing. Yet despite all its injuries, it continued on, not slowing as it ran deeper into the forest. It completely ignored the men as it disappeared into the dense brush. Even after it was out of earshot, Obadiah waited two minutes before breaking the silence.

"...Let's head back. Quickly now! No reason to tempt fate."

Cyrus cracked the whip. The stray goat bolted to join the herd. Not one minute later, another goat fell out of line, so Cyrus swung the whip again. This time of year there were twelve hours of sunlight each day, and Horace'd be damned if he didn't keep the caravan moving for at least eleven of 'em. And within the past eleven and a half hours of traveling, Cyrus never got more than five minute's rest before one of the flock needed correction. His arm had never been more tired.

When Lemuel's horse strode alongside Cyrus', his despair finally faded. Lemuel spoke the words that were sweet music to Cyrus' ears. "We'll be stopping to set up camp soon."

Cyrus was too exhausted to speak, so he tied the whip to the saddle and nodded as he and Lemuel rode their horses to where the wagons were stopped. Lemuel looked at Cyrus smugly and said, "Not so easy when you don't have Spot doin' all the work, huh?"

"Yeah," Cyrus said. "I guess I know what it was like for you now."

Lemuel opened his mouth to reply, but stopped as if remembering something suddenly. Then he spoke much more quietly. "Fido never helped me out as much as your Spot did, but I still miss him dearly."

Cyrus winced. "I'm sorry, Lemuel. I didn't make it in time to help Fido."

"It's not your fault. I'm grateful that you tried. I didn't even bother. I kept telling myself, 'Just because that thing got Cyrus' dog don't mean it got yours; Fido will turn up any minute.' But I knew it wasn't true. I was just too scared."

They rode their horses onward until the density of people setting up camp made it necessary to find a place to hitch their mounts. Lemuel went off to his family while Cyrus made his way to where people were already preparing the cauldron for stew. Among the crowd of people waiting and talking, he was approached by Jemima.

"How was ridin' today, Cyrus?" she asked.

"Terrible. How's Spot holdin' up?"

"He's doin' much better!" Jemima smiled. "I couldn't believe the state he was in when you got 'im out of that cave a week ago. But his injuries are nearly healed already."

"That's a relief," said Cyrus. "Thank you for takin' care of him and letting him ride in your wagon with you an' Nellie."

"Of course!" Jemima said. "But there's one other thing. I only noticed it today, but I think Nellie is pregnant!"

"She is?!" exclaimed Cyrus. "That's good news! But wait. Who do you think could be — ya know..."

"Well, you should see how Nellie and Spot have been nuzzling up with each other over the past few days! I think he's the father."

"Really? He musta been seeing her behind Fido's back. Quite the hound, ain't he?"

"My, my. How scandalous!" Jemima said, before they both burst into laughter.

Jemima continued once they caught their breath. "You should really visit him, Cyrus. I don't know why you haven't wanted to see your dog over the past few days."

Cyrus sighed. "I know, I know. It's just... It felt terrible to see the state he was in with his injuries. Seeing how it was all my fault."

"Your fault? You saved Spot!"

"But maybe he wouldn't have gotten taken in the first place had I been paying better attention."

Jemima huffed. "You couldn't have kept Spot from being taken any better than Lemeul could've protected Fido. Besides, like I said, he's nearly all better now. The only wound that hasn't healed yet is the bite mark on his neck. He's doing fine. Even had a growth spurt!"

Cyrus looked up. "A growth spurt?"

"Yep. He's much bigger now! And here I thought he was all done growing."

"He is," Cyrus said. "Or he should be. Doesn't this seem odd to you?"

"Well I don't know," Jemima said. "Some dogs grow to be pretty big, right?"

Cyrus looked contemplative as he replied. "Actually... I think I will go see him. 'Bout time I gave him a visit."

"Good!" Jemima pointed. "Spot and Nellie are both in my wagon down that-a-way. I'll stay here and save a bowl o' stew for ya."

Cyrus began to walk with haste as he tried to ignore the uneasy feeling in his gut. A few folks tried to flag him down about dinner being ready soon, but he waved them off and kept going. The sun was setting, and the sky was growing darker. After a moment, he arrived at the wagon. He climbed up, pulled back the curtain, and entered.

The wagon was empty. Jemima's stuff sat in a few bags in the corner, and the opposite corner held a folded rug and some old rags and torn clothing, all of which were covered in dog hair. He figured that it must be what the dogs had been using as a bed. Cyrus poked his head out of the wagon. From this vantage point, he could see them out in the grassy field.

Spot *had* grown. He was bigger than Jemima said he'd be.

His fur was matted and wild, longer in some places than others. The bite marks on his neck were still there, swollen and inflamed. The muscles of his forelegs were sturdy and knotted. His jaws and teeth looked like they belonged on a bear. And in his mouth, he held Nellie by the nape of her neck.

Spot always used to look at Cyrus with love and adoration, but when their eyes met, they were cold, fierce, and held no recognition. Cyrus was gripped by a hollowness that froze him in place, and before he could decide what to do, he noticed something else watching him.

Standing at the very top of a distant tree, there was... a man? Its silhouette was shaded by the ever darkening sky, but it seemed to be wrapped in a cloak. Its eyes were a brilliant, bright red.

Cyrus turned his attention back to Spot, but he was now facing away from him in the direction of the treeline.

"...Spot." Cyrus had tried to shout it, but his voice caught in his throat. It still should have been loud enough for Spot to hear. But instead of reacting, Spot began to run without looking back.

The red-eyed man's cloak billowed behind him, and it expanded into two huge, insectile wings. It turned and flew out of sight over the canopy just as Spot disappeared into the forest, dragging Nellie as he went.

EPILOGUE

MATT DWINELL

"Well, Mothy, you seem to have brought along some mighty scrumptious waif errors. Which ones can I eat?" My leathery-winged rival and I looked down at the sleeping settlement of covered wagons.

"None of them, Jersey. You see, they all made it California-way safely." Maybe we'd lost a few here and there from my new friend, Sam the Worm and the Wildman. And well, there was that wolf-dog and the Lake monster and the tornado thing. But the number of humans seemed right- numbers being a human concept- and Jersey didn't need to know about the little mishaps on the way.

"Mothy, are you telling me that not a one of the fragile human folk dropped dead on their journey out here? That it's not a ship of thezpians situation?"

"What's a ship of thezpians?"

"You wouldn't understand."

"Jersey, it's true! I would never understand your culture.

But I *do* understand you owe me a couple of casks of your finest."

Jersey's face got tight and angry, and for a moment, he glanced down at the lead wagon. Drool dripped down his red cheeks. "Perhaps if I eat just one, then it's you who owes me the best of the Scuppernong."

"Uh-uh-uh." I held up the contract that Jersey had put his mark on. "Says here, claws three-bee. No interfering."

Jersey got all grouchy like he tends to do when folk in a civilized utopolosis can't see his tantrums.

"Fine. You win this one. But I wager I could take twice this number back east with nary a scratch on them."

Jersey could be a brash devil with no impulse control.

"Same terms?" I asked.

He growled in assent. We shook hoof to paw on the hill while my travelers slept on safe and mostly sound.

ABOUT THE AUTHORS

Amiee Nwabuike

Amiee Nwabuike lives in Raleigh with no pets. Instead, she has a collection of half-eaten jars of almond butter—much to her loved ones' distress. She writes mostly comedy and fantasy and enjoys giving her readers tales to disturb and delight. She currently has no plans to go West, but one day, she would like to make the journey to Point Pleasant to touch Mothman's butt.

Antonio Dinkens

Antonio Dinkens lives in Raleigh with no pets, but many plants. He enjoys writing queer and black stories with the touch of magical realism. When not writing he pursues a number of hobbies from dungeons and dragons to the newer found one of Brazilian Jiu-Jitsu.

David Badenchini

David Badenchini lives in Charlotte. He enjoys writing fantasy to scifi to whatever supernatural fits in between.

Eerie Maeyflower

Eerie was lambasted for not using her real name for this anthology, but she spent a lot of time and energy trying to find a Gmail handle that wasn't taken, so the others will have to deal with her decision. She enjoys long walks on days that are not too hot and not too cold (essentially 7 days out of the year). Her diet consists mainly of sushi, so she really needs her writing career to take off if she's going to maintain this lifestyle.

Gabriel Peragine

Gabriel Peragine is a creative located in Garner with his two fur children and his husband. When he's not writing, he's working on his unreleased fantasy webcomic or binging horror flicks. You can find his art on Instagram at @pairojeanart

Matthew Dwinell

Matthew Dwinell writes speculative fiction of all sorts whenever he's not engrossed in any of his many other hobbies. A hopeless nerd, he lives in Cary with his partner and two cats (one princess, and one gremlin). He loves exploring how our imaginations can map mystery and wonder onto this world—and isn't that what cryptids are all about?

ACKNOWLEDGMENTS

Thank you to the Cary Writing Critique group for your support in helping us craft better stories. We'd also like to thank Dawn for her edits and educating us on "towards" vs "toward", and Angel for bringing our characters to life on the cover of this anthology.

www.ingramcontent.com/pod-product-compliance
Ingram Content Group UK Ltd.
Pitfield, Milton Keynes, MK11 3LW, UK
UKHW041825200726
13854UKWH00002BA/563

9 798218 938215